WE LIGHT UP
THE SKY

Also by Lilliam Rivera

Never Look Back

WE LIGHT UP THE SKY

Lilliam Rivera

BLOOMSBURY

NEW YORK   LONDON   OXFORD   NEW DELHI   SYDNEY

BLOOMSBURY YA
Bloomsbury Publishing Inc., part of Bloomsbury Publishing Plc
1385 Broadway, New York, NY 10018

BLOOMSBURY and the Diana logo are trademarks of Bloomsbury Publishing Plc

First published in the United States of America in October 2021 by Bloomsbury YA

Bloomsbury books may be purchased for business or promotional use.
For information on bulk purchases please contact Macmillan Corporate and
Premium Sales Department at specialmarkets@macmillan.com

Library of Congress Cataloging-in-Publication Data
Names: Rivera, Lilliam, author.
Title: We light up the sky / by Lilliam Rivera.
Description: New York : Bloomsbury Children's Books, 2021.
Summary: Three Latinx teenagers struggle to deal with encounters with an alien,
and try to warn the world of the possibility of an alien invasion.
Identifiers: LCCN 2021018094 (print) | LCCN 2021018095 (e-book)
ISBN 978-1-5476-0376-3 (hardcover) • ISBN 978-1-5476-0377-0 (e-book)
Subjects: CYAC: Extraterrestrial beings—Fiction. | Hispanic Americans—Fiction. |
Social classes—Fiction. | Survival—Fiction. | Los Angeles (Calif.)—Fiction.
Classification: LCC PZ7.1.R5765 We 2021 (print) | LCC PZ7.1.R5765 (e-book) |
DDC [Fic]—dc23
LC record available at https://lccn.loc.gov/2021018094

Book design by Jeanette Levy
Typeset by Westchester Publishing Services
Printed and bound in the U.S.A.
2 4 6 8 10 9 7 5 3 1

To find out more about our authors and books visit
www.bloomsbury.com and sign up for our newsletters.

To all the young people saving this world,
in spite of it all

WE LIGHT UP
THE SKY

CHAPTER 1

Five days before the Visitor lands, Pedro has an unusual encounter at the bus stop where he always waits for the 7 a.m. bus to take him to Fairfax High. There's a dense morning fog that sweeps across the streets adding to Pedro's drowsiness. Last night he went to La Plaza to watch Kandi perform. It was the late Rocío Dúrcal's birthday, and Kandi was deep in his emotions. The flawless performer lip-synched to "Amor Eterno" with tears streaming down his immaculately painted face. Pedro sat at his usual corner table in awe of the emotional display, so much so that he too succumbed to a tear or two.

Pedro's not technically allowed in the twenty-one-and-over club, but La Plaza has been his sometime home for so long that the owner overlooks his age. La Plaza is the only place Pedro feels safe, and because of that, Pedro frequently stays out way too late. But he's never tardy to school no matter how many times the club calls to him. He would never allow his "misguided antics" to get in the way of showing out academically and aesthetically.

Dressed in a combination of his two favorite stunners—pop star Kali Uchis and the principe de chocolate Andrés from the only television show that counts, *Los Espookys*—Pedro looks primed to battle any drama in sequin joggers and blue high-tops. Or, at the very least, to almost pass this morning's history test. What he didn't expect was a beastly run-in at the bus stop.

Pedro barely pays attention to what he thinks is a stray dog until the wild animal slowly comes into focus. The coyote's fur is knotted in between bald spots. Its snout is long, and one of its pointy ears has a stripe of white. The animal looks hungry.

"Híjole," Pedro whispers.

The coyote stares at him, and Pedro is still. This is a dog, an ancient dog, who will sense Pedro's fear if he shows it, so he doesn't. By some miracle he decided not to blast Kali Uchis in his eardrums, something he normally does when he walks by himself. At least he can hear if the coyote starts running after him to tear his heart out or whatever it is coyotes do to measly humans.

"You don't want this," he says.

The animal seems to take in Pedro's glittery pants and the black T-shirt that lists *Los Espookys* cast names: "Renaldo y Andrés y Ursula y Tati y Tico." It draws nearer. Pedro doesn't notice the flower protruding from the side of the coyote's rib cage. It is as if the animal has brushed up against a blooming plant sometime during its travel, embedding the head within its dirty coat.

Pedro knows he should run, but where? The garage

behind him is closed, and the apartment complex across the street is too far away to make a difference. The beast would be on top of him even before he made it there. He's sure of it.

"Leave me be, ancient perra," Pedro says quietly as the coyote takes a couple of steps forward. Fear rises, starting from his toes, inching up to Pedro's stomach. The coyote doesn't stop. It gradually comes closer.

A car suddenly takes a sharp turn onto the street. The coyote calmly turns away from Pedro and struts into the dense fog. Pedro glares in disbelief until the dog disappears.

Why is a coyote trying to kill me this morning? reads the caption Pedro writes on the 'gram with a picture of the foggy street. Pedro has ten thousand followers, but he thinks it's really low considering the quality content he posts. Pedro's not a TikToker although he should make the transition. He just refuses to do so.

Before he boards the bus, a hundred followers hit the heart button on his post.

While most people who aren't originally from Los Angeles may think the city is nothing but a daily dose of sunshine and organic food, those like Pedro understand the coyote is a reminder of how no one truly belongs here. Not the recent transplants. Not even Pedro, who was born in the heart of the City of Angels.

The beastly encounter was a first for Pedro. *Today is going to be something, isn't it?* he thinks. He rechecks his horoscopes (Astro Poets, CHANI, Co-Star) to confirm if there are any ominous signs he should be aware of. His Leo horoscope in Astro Poets is the one he obsesses over the most: *Expect the unexpected. Be open to new encounters. Denim, perhaps? Light a hot-pink candle.*

As he boards the bus, Pedro doesn't notice the tiny petals sprinkled on the street, left behind by the coyote.

The horoscopes have spoken. Whoever is supposed to show up this week—hot girl, boy, or person—better be ready to shower this Leo with love, not mayhem. And take note: I am open to Diptyque candles and designer jeans, he writes.

The image Pedro posts is one of his face tilted against the bus window to show off his strong jawline and lips that have a hint of pink to them. He flashes a sexy smile.

✳ ✳ ✳

In a stately house located in historic West Adams, Luna eats her bowl of oatmeal, leaning over the kitchen island. She still feels unsettled from last night's nightmare. In her recurring dream, she's in the hospital trying desperately to see her cousin before it's too late. With each step she takes, LAPD stops her, takes her temperature, and asks her inane questions. As she tries to break through their barriers, her desperation escalates. She yells at the sunglass-wearing man in uniform, and he pushes her to the ground over and over until a door in a long, desolate hallway unlocks. Luna runs toward the room, away from the menacing cops, but when she finally reaches the eerie hospital bed, she finds a body hidden under a sheet. With trembling hands, Luna gradually pulls off the bedsheet, only to wake up before confirming who lies there.

The heavy bags under her eyes reflect off the toaster. She made them worse by trying to conceal the tiredness with makeup.

"Horrible," she says to herself. Luna takes out the picture of her cousin she keeps tucked in her schoolbag. Tasha had dyed her shoulder-length hair purplish pink. She wanted Luna to change her hair color too, to update her usual dark brown hair to something more fun. But Luna doesn't like change. Tasha teased her for being such a moody Cancer.

The aftereffects of the disturbing dream are like tiny jabs. She thought keeping herself busy would help stave off these heavy emotions. This week, it will be two years since Tasha died. Two years. How is it even possible? Her life was forever altered that day.

"You're looking cute."

Her mother enters the kitchen in her nurses' scrubs and yellow clogs. Luna puts away the picture.

"Thanks. Spirit week," she says. Everyone at school is meant to wear pink today. Never one to go against the grain, Luna wears a pastel pink silk top with tights and ankle boots.

Luna's mother pours coffee into her Rambler. She smiles, and Luna tries to return the gesture, but it feels disingenuous. Luna hasn't been talking to her mother this past month, at least not with any kind of depth. Not that she's angry at her. She's just been focusing on school and burying her feelings.

5

"Don't forget to take the garbage out tonight," her mother says.

Luna's face drops. What is she even talking about? This week is not a normal week. Doesn't she remember?

"I thought we were going to drive to the cemetery after school," Luna says, trying hard to keep her voice from shaking. She hates feeling this way, like she needs help. Like she's weak.

"I'm pulling a double shift, covering for two nurses," her mother says. "We'll go the following weekend. We'll make a day of it. I promise."

This week needs to be perfect. Her mother brushing it off only brings into focus how much she doesn't care. Why are strangers more important to her than her own daughter? Why can't she see how Tasha was supposed to be here with her? Instead, Luna has to deal with everything on her own, with no one to share every silly thing, every secret, every joy.

When her mother reaches out to her, Luna moves away.

"I'm leaving in five minutes." Her mother sighs. "You ready?"

"Yes." Luna rinses her bowl in the kitchen sink and places it in the dishwasher. She grabs her backpack and follows her mother to the car.

"Can we not listen to music? I have to study," Luna says. The radio is reluctantly turned off.

"Honey, I heard you last night. Everything okay?"

Luna concentrates on her textbook. Does she tell her about the nightmare? How she woke up crying? She misses Tasha so much, and her mother just seems unmoved. Honestly, no one is interested. So she keeps this heartache to herself.

"Yes, everything is fine," Luna says. "I had a nightmare, that's all."

Luna's mother nervously taps on the steering wheel. "Do you want Ceci to keep you company tonight while I work? What do you think?"

Ceci and her mom both work at the hospital, and she lives five minutes away. Luna likes Ceci well enough, but she doesn't want to talk to her. Ceci is into feeling your emotions and talking them through. She gifted Luna a journal to write down her "morning pages." The journal is still on Luna's bedside, unopened.

"I'm going to be studying," Luna says. Her mother doesn't press the subject. They drive in silence until they reach the school drop-off.

"Have a good day, baby."

This week is going to be a continuation of the past two years, just a deep well of sadness.

"Thanks, Mom," Luna says as she opens the car door and joins the rest of the students marching toward campus.

* * *

Rafa doesn't have money for the bus, so he walks along the wide Wilshire Boulevard, heading west. The daily journey takes him an hour and a half, and his sneakers are barely holding up, what with all the walking he's been doing ever since he started attending Fairfax. He'll have to replace them soon.

His backpack holds the drawing his sister, Mónica, gave him this morning. The crinkled paper depicts the moon and stars, and on one of the stars, she drew a little house with a chimney bellowing smoke. Rafa asked her if she knew what that was, considering she's never been to a home with a working fireplace.

"It's where we are going to live," she said. "It's called Casa Estrella. Lots of families will live there."

Mónica is missing her two front teeth, so whenever she talks, there is a pronounced lisp, and when she frowns, she looks like an abuela. Rafa doesn't tell her that, though. He doesn't want her to be sensitive about her ghost teeth.

He enters the school through a side entrance, early enough to eat the free breakfast, which he does, although the burrito is bland and the tortilla tastes as if it's been refrigerated for too long. Soon the first bell rings. He gathers his things then heads to homeroom. His jean jacket is frayed and full of holes. It doesn't offer much warmth. He digs his hands deep in the pockets of his dusty black jeans.

The classroom slowly fills with students, none of whom speak to Rafa. He started at Fairfax three weeks ago, a late transfer into the senior year class, and it seems nobody had room for new friends. He sniffs at his jean jacket. It smells dirty.

"Don't worry losers, I've arrived!" Pedro announces as he enters the room and saunters over to the seat in front of Rafa. Rafa doesn't make a comment, though in his mind he tells a witty joke and imagines Pedro enjoying it. He absentmindedly stares at Pedro's sequin jogging pants. He thinks of the brilliance of stars and how they appeared last night when he stepped out of the tent.

Rafa and his family have been living underneath the highway ramp for a couple of months now. Before the tent, they lived in a converted garage. When the owners told his family they had to vacate because someone had called the city, they were really apologetic. The news couldn't have come at a worse time—his father was just let go at the car wash. The tent is a temporary solution until his father finds a new job. Temporary, like everything in Rafa's life. His worn sneakers. The hair he doesn't have money to cut professionally, so it just grows unruly. The stench from his jean jacket.

If he studies Pedro's dazzling pants, then maybe Rafa can forget about the long walk home and how his sleeping bag doesn't keep him warm enough.

"You're in my seat."

His name is Isaac, and ever since Rafa began attending Fairfax, Isaac has been on him. Rafa stays focused on the sequins.

"You didn't hear me," Isaac says. "Get your fat ass off my seat."

There hasn't been a fight between them yet, but it seems inevitable. Isaac won't stop until Rafa sheds blood, a tear, or both.

He slowly looks up.

"Did you forget to finish off your witches' brew this morning?" Rafa says.

Pedro turns around and cackles.

"Witches' brew!" Pedro says. "That's some funny Shakespearean shade."

"Did he just call me a bitch?" Isaac asks Luna, who stands behind him.

Luna laughs. "It sounds like it," she says and takes her seat by Rafa.

Frustrated, Isaac grabs Rafa by the collar of his jean jacket. The classroom erupts. It's going down, and everyone seems eager to see a fight happen. No one knows the quiet new kid, but they all know Isaac.

"You heard me."

"Everyone on this planet heard you. No one cares," Rafa whispers so only Isaac can hear. Isaac's ears turn red.

"Gentlemen!"

The homeroom teacher, Mr. Alvarez, enters the classroom.

"Seats. Now."

Isaac quickly drops Rafa's jacket. They glare at each other, and for those few seconds, Rafa understands this moment will not end here.

"I'll see you later," Isaac says and walks to the back of the room to sit with his buddies.

"And that concludes today's riveting insight into toxic masculinity," Pedro says into his phone. Then he swerves the camera to Rafa. "Thanks in part to him."

"You're welcome," Rafa says quietly. "I guess."

Beside him, Luna shifts in her chair.

While Mr. Alvarez takes attendance, Rafa hears Isaac talking about him. He glances at the clock hanging on the wall. It's not even 9 a.m. and today is already too much.

✳ ✳ ✳

Somewhere in space, the Visitor approaches earth.

CHAPTER 2

"Isaac keeps asking about you." Soledad's round face is all eagerness.

"Annnnnnd?" Luna drags the letter *n* as long as she can.

Right before Tasha died, Isaac and Luna hung out. It wasn't anything serious, not on her part anyway. Because of the lockdown, it wasn't safe to meet with people, but they found ways to connect. Her mother was too busy at the hospital to notice, and everything felt so chaotic during that time. The relationship elevated to sex once, but it was just sad sex. Luna wanted to feel something other than despair, and Isaac happened to be around. It was a selfish mistake. Isaac constantly pursuing her reminds Luna of that painful period.

"No reason." Soledad twirls her hair around her long, gelled nails. They're transparent with white "clouds" painted on top. Most girls are sporting the same trendy color except for Luna. Tasha would be so grossed out if she saw her bare nails. Luna is falling behind on appearances. She needs to do better.

"He's still into you. You can tell," Soledad adds with what sounds like a hint of jealousy.

Luna closes her locker. Soledad is part of the group that includes Isaac and most of the football team and the cheerleaders. Luna's not sure if she even likes Soledad or the others. What the group is into—smoking, sex, drama—Luna simply isn't, but she pretends to be. It's just easier that way. She goes along with them instead of drowning in the depths of her grief. It may be exhausting to act as if she cares whether or not Isaac likes her, but it's better than the alternative. So Luna displays a grin.

"Did you see the way he got into the new boy's face?" Luna asks.

Soledad laughs, and Luna lazily joins her. They walk toward their next class.

Luna noticed Rafa the first day he arrived at school. Rafa has what Tasha would've called "sad eyes," as if he's on the verge of tears. Sometimes Luna imagines the conversation she would have had with Tasha about the new boy:

"He's hot, but he probably knows it," Luna says.

"You're already in love. I can tell." Tasha pokes Luna in the ribs.

"Shut up, that's not true."

"Stick with Isaac."

"Been there, done that," Luna says, bored.

"So, do it again!" And then they would both cackle like witches.

Luna can't have any of these conversations with Soledad. She doesn't feel safe, like her words might be misconstrued in some way.

"I think Isaac is planning to kick his ass after school," Soledad says with glee.

Luna doesn't want Isaac to kick anyone's ass, especially the quiet boy with beautiful brown eyes, but she won't say. She doesn't want to lose whatever it is she has with this group of friends. Without them, she would truly be alone.

"He should wait until the field trip," Soledad says.

"What field trip?" Luna asks.

"The field trip. This Friday?"

"What are you talking about?" The hallway is so crowded with students trying to make it to their classes before the late bell rings. Almost everyone says hi to them. Luna waves back.

"Luna, we're going to the Griffith Observatory on Friday. The whole class."

No, that's not possible. The last time Luna went to the observatory was with her cousin. They smoked weed, watched the laser show, and spoke about the future, one of their last deep conversations. This was before Tasha got sick, before life became a dark abyss. Observatories were Tasha's favorite places to visit.

"No, I'm not doing that."

"You don't have a choice," Soledad says. "We're getting graded."

Luna vowed never to visit an observatory again, not without Tasha. This is not going to happen.

"I need to speak to the teacher," she says.

"Right now? We're going to be late to math," Soledad warns. Luna pushes against the mass of students toward where the science teacher Mrs. Delgado stands outside of her classroom, greeting each entering student.

"Ladies, we're not meeting today," Mrs. Delgado says.

"I won't be able to attend the field trip."

Luna's mother taught her how to speak to people of authority, to affirm her statements instead of asking for permission.

"It's fifty percent of your grade for this quarter," Mrs. Delgado says.

"Half our grade! That's not fair." Her whole body tenses as she scrambles to find the right words that won't betray her. "One field trip shouldn't take up so much of our grade. And I shouldn't have to justify my personal reasons."

Her voice gets louder. Mrs. Delgado doesn't like to be argued with. It's not the way you get things done with her. Luna knows this, but she can't stop herself.

"I can make up the grade with other work." She clutches her textbook tight enough to display the whites of her knuckles.

"You are more than welcome to opt out of the trip. The outcome still stands," Mrs. Delgado says, allowing one last student to enter the room. "The bell is about to ring. I suggest you two head to your next class."

Seconds go by. Luna wants to continue stating her

case, but there's no point. Mrs. Delgado never budges, not even for Soledad, who seems to have a way of convincing teachers to fix her low grades. It has something to do with her father being the former mayor and a Fairfax graduate.

Mrs. Delgado closes the door. The bell goes off.

"I can't believe this," Luna says.

"At least you tried, but I could have told you not to bother," Soledad says with a chuckle. Luna tries to temper her rage. She shouldn't have to explain to a teacher or anyone why she doesn't want to go. Observatories are sacred places to her, like the ones in Puerto Rico and Hawaii she visited with Tasha. Luna doesn't want her memories of those moments to be tarnished, trampled by others.

Pedro roughly bumps into Soledad in the near-empty hallway.

"Watch yourself, perras!" he yells at them.

"God, I hate him," Soledad says. "We hate you, perra!"

The girls are late to class, but Soledad uses her charm to convince the teacher to ignore the tardiness.

Luna tries to concentrate on the lesson, but she's so mad. How did she manage to block the trip completely from her mind? She's been so hyper-focused on getting to the cemetery. She can't even do that now. Her mother is once again pushing off the visit like it's no big deal. Can't she see how important this is to Luna? It's the least she could do for her cousin, to see the place that marks her end.

"Promise me."

Luna gasps at the sudden sound of Tasha's voice in her head. Tasha's final words to her. She spirals back to that painful phone call, her hands suddenly clammy. Luna's no longer in the classroom but in the past with Tasha's voice reminding her how terrible of a cousin she is. A promise she failed to keep. The guilt is unbearable.

"Luna, can you come up to the board and show us how we arrive to this answer?" her precalculus teacher calls, and brings her back to the present. Luna rapidly blinks to keep a tear from escaping.

She goes up and explains her formula to the class. It's an automatic response. She can easily tackle problems with concrete answers. Theorems and absolute values. It's the other subjects that trip her up, especially when they ask her to shed her hard shell and reveal herself on the page. Her AP English teacher loves to do that. History too. Luna prefers numbers.

"Good work. Who has the answer to problem five?"

Tasha was the complete opposite of Luna. She would express her every emotion on paper. Although she loved science as much as Luna did, her passion for astronomy was more akin to romance. The idea of infinite possibilities. But the vastness of space scares Luna. Math, you can control. There is a right or wrong answer. But the sky? The clouds? The wind? There is no way of controlling them.

The one constant in Luna's life is how much she misses Tasha. This school trip will only bring her heartache to the surface. Tasha died so suddenly, but back then, so many were dying. Most people didn't expect the young to be affected by COVID-19, least of all Luna. The virus hit Tasha's parents first. They all thought her young cousin would recover like her mom and dad. But she didn't.

✳ ✳ ✳

After school Luna gets a ride from Soledad, who drives her father's Prius. The car looks new except for the dent Soledad made when she tried squeezing into a compact car space.

"Let's go to Nonna's," Soledad says. A cute guy works the register, and Soledad has been trying to get his attention. Luna agrees to go.

"I'll have the Cuban and the carne asada," Luna says. Soledad continues to chat with the guy, who seems to like the attention but not love it.

"Isaac and the rest of them are asking where we are at," Soledad says after finally pulling herself away.

"I need to get home soon," Luna says. "It's okay if you can't take me. I'll take the bus."

"The bus! Jesus, Luna. You're not starting that again, being all Ms. Doom?" Soledad says. "You've been with that face ever since I mentioned the field trip."

"No, no, I'm not," Luna quickly says. It wasn't too long ago when Soledad told Luna she needed to live and stop being so miserable all the time.

"Everyone is a little tired of it," she had said.

Luna heard her loud and clear. She's been trying to keep her sadness at bay, to not reveal it. But with the news of the trip, she just wants to retreat and hide.

To prove she's over it, Luna types their location into the group chat. Within a few minutes, their table is surrounded by boys.

"Can I have a bite?" Isaac asks.

"You wish." Luna eats the last of her empanada.

"You're so cold, Luna."

"No, I'm not," she says with a grin.

When she hooked up with Isaac, he was very sweet. She felt so distraught during that time. Isaac would let her cry quietly and not bombard her with questions. Instead, he held her and was gentle. Isaac has slight dimples that reveal themselves when he smiles, like right now. Most of the girls in school swear he looks like a tall Jaden Smith. Luna said it was only physical. So maybe he's right. She *is* cold. Luna offers him a sip of her soda.

"It's getting late," she says, this time more urgently.

They walk toward Soledad's parked car.

"You going to the school trip?" Isaac asks.

"I don't have much of a choice."

"Of course you have a choice." He lowers his voice. "We can ditch and hang out. Just you and me."

It would be so easy. Tasha would have told her to say yes. But Tasha is not here, and Luna is stuck in this in-between state where her "friends" are not the friends she craves and her world is not aligned to what she needs. An in-between state where she's surrounded by grief.

Where her cousin is nowhere and everywhere. There is no expiration date for her mourning, and yet those around her believe her sorrow should have ended months ago.

"We haven't hung out in a long time," Isaac says.

It would be so simple.

"I'll think about it," Luna says. He opens the car door for her, and she slides in. Isaac punches his friend in the arm for trying to get in the back seat. They play fight, causing enough noise bystanders get annoyed. Soledad cheers them on, and Luna joins in.

A strange light blankets the sky. Luna doesn't notice it, and neither do any of her friends.

CHAPTER 3

Pedro skates up Fairfax Avenue, swerving away from sneaker heads toting their precious loads of overpriced trainers. His phone is in front of his face.

"So many beautiful creatures out today," he says. "Too bad they're too busy looking at sneaks."

He stops at the corner of Clinton and posts the story. It's not his finest content, but it will have to do for now. He has to get to In-N-Out before his shift begins. Pedro wants to hit La Plaza on Friday and doesn't want to waste money taking the bus. His skateboard will get him to work just fine.

A group of Fairfax students congregate across the street from Pedro. No one offers him a ride. Instead, they honk their horns or flash their middle fingers at him. If they were smart, they would drive him to work. He's a great conversationalist.

"You may be young, but you can hold your own in all types of circles." That's what the owner of La Plaza said to him once. Funny, that's not what his Uncle Benji thinks.

Uncle Benji thinks Pedro is good for nothing. He hates everything about him: his sequin joggers, the type of music he listens to, and definitely his Instagram account.

It's a ridiculous cliché. Poor Mama alone without a man. Her brother pops in to check on her whenever he feels like it. Uncle Benji screams at his mom, telling her how she's doing it all wrong, raising Pedro to fail. Why does Pedro dress the way he does? Why is he out every weekend? Why is he posting crap online instead of working? Why? Why? Why?

When Pedro defends himself, things inevitably turn ugly. Mom cries in Spanish. Pedro wails in both languages, and then he's out the door for days on end, couch or floor surfing until his uncle leaves. Uncle Benji is due to return soon. He never gives a warning when. Why should he when he has his own key to the house? After each one of his visits, Pedro threatens to leave his mom forever. Her tears convince him not to.

"Give me a ride, puto?" Pedro yells across the street to a friend from English class. "You need me to give you that extra glow your pale face lacks."

The boy shakes his head and laughs.

Pedro continues up Fairfax toward Sunset. There is a slight hill, and he's getting a little out of breath. Girls in sports bras walk their dogs. He smiles at one of them. "I see you, Ivy Park."

The girl smiles back.

"It's dark already, so the vampires are slowly emerging," Pedro says in his IG live. The hearts pop up on the feed, and it warms him. It's a clear night. No clouds in the sky.

Once he reaches Sunset, Pedro bends his knees and takes a right toward Highland. He found the skateboard on Fairfax one day. Probably someone got too high to remember where they left it. Pedro spotted it behind a mailbox and just rode off. No one stopped him.

"I have arrived," Pedro says when he enters the already bustling In-N-Out. The place is crowded with Hollywood High students and tourists. Always tourists.

He heads to the back room and quickly changes into his uniform. He washes his hands and face thoroughly.

"Hi, Espooky." His coworker Melissa saddles up to him by the sink. "You ready?"

"Ready to deal with annoying customers ordering from a secret menu?" he says. "No."

Melissa taps her back pocket. "¿Quieres?"

Pedro says no to her flask of vodka. Melissa likes being toasted during her shift. Pedro doesn't judge. He tried to work once after taking a tab of E. Although he was super affectionate to everyone, even the customers, he didn't really like it. Pedro's not into drugs or drinking. He likes being fully alert in this life.

He places the drive-through microphone over his head. "What do you think? Do I look like LaBritney?"

"You look like someone who works at In-N-Out."

He sticks his tongue out, and they both go to their respective stations. Pedro outside and Melissa to the counter.

23

A lot of his coworkers don't like drive-through duties, but Pedro prefers it over working inside. He likes seeing people, being right in the action. When it's a good day, a friend or two from La Plaza will emerge and he's reminded of his other life where he is fully seen. He makes sure they get extra fries. It's the least he can do.

"Welcome to In-N-Out. How may I help you?" he says to the driver of a BMW. When the driver rolls down the window, a big whiff of weed pours out.

"I want a veggie burrito," a girl inside the car says then laughs.

Pedro has seen the boy around Fairfax before. He's a rich sneaker head who always has the latest brand on his feet. His eyes are a cold blue. Pedro grins and waits for him to begin.

"She wants a burrito," the boy says.

"You must be lost. This is In-N-Out, and we make the best burgers," Pedro says. "I can help you with a burger and fries, a milkshake."

"She wants a burrito. You know what I'm talking about." He leans out of his car to tap on Pedro's order tablet. "Burritos, quesadillas. That Mexican shit."

Pedro lets out a long sigh. This is so boring. How ridiculous white people are behind their expensive cars. Being racist because they think it's funny or will get them laid or whatever.

"Would you like to place an order?" Pedro says as sweetly as possible. The car behind this one inches forward.

"I've seen you around," the boy says.

Pedro covers the microphone so his bosses are unable to hear him.

"Of course you have. I've entered your dreams whenever you call me by my name," Pedro says. "Remember, like last night?"

The girl cackles. Pedro leans farther in to the car.

"You remember too, don't you?" Pedro addresses the girl. "When you called me papi?"

The boy with the cold, blue eyes grows nervous while the girl beside him practically chokes.

"We want number two, extra-toasted bun with two chocolate milkshakes," the boy finally says.

"And fries with cheese."

Pedro taps into his pad and sends in the order. "Thank you. I hope you have a blessed night."

The couple drives forward. Pedro notices how the boy continues to check him out in his rearview mirror.

Yeah, bitch, you've seen me before, Pedro thinks. *I'm unforgettable.*

"People out here trying to act like they aren't racist, homophobic pieces of basura," Pedro speaks into his microphone. On the other end is Eduardo, who goes to Hollywood High and hates working at the fast food restaurant. Eduardo never engages with Pedro on these rants. Pedro continues anyway. "Eduardo, do you copy? Because I need an acknowledgment on what I'm saying."

"Yes, Pedro, I copy," Eduardo says. "Can you just keep it moving? The line is spilling out onto the street."

"What would you like to order?" Pedro says to the next customer.

A coyote encounter and now this. Pedro thinks the gods and goddesses are trying to tell him something. But what? His plan is to stay out as long as possible so when he gets home, his mom will be asleep and he won't have to hear how bad things are, how the unpaid bills are stacking up, and the other usual dramas.

The next row of cars goes on without any incident. Melissa eventually comes out to relieve him, and he heads to the break room to eat. He can't stop thinking about that blue-eyed devil. No matter how many witty comebacks he gets in, Pedro still feels the words are never enough to make a difference. The things he would do to their food if he were that type of a person . . .

Pedro's shift ends without any interruptions, and the bus ride home is also uneventful. He spends the time answering DMs from various people. Collaborations to work with unknown brands. When will the Guccis and the Versaces send him a message? He posts a photo dump, a lazy post if ever there was one, and engages with a couple of the comments. Being socially active is a job. Adoration, however light it may seem, is still something he can hold on to.

Good night, my loves. Tomorrow we ride, he types as the bus approaches his stop. Pedro grabs his skateboard and leisurely walks home. All he wants is sleep. Tomorrow is another day of school and work. He thinks of what he will wear. Something bright and loud might shake off this drabness.

26

"Fuck me."

Uncle Benji's car is parked in the driveway, and Pedro must make a decision. Avoid entering a hostile situation, or move forward with the hope that this time it will be different. From where he stands, he watches his mother flit about in the kitchen, probably heating up food. It's way past nine o'clock, and Uncle Benji is already disrupting their home.

Ever since his uncle opened another garage in Maywood, he's been spending way more time in their house, acting as if he owns it. Pedro's mom never objects, what with groceries and certain bills being paid. But not Pedro. He can't take it.

Pedro inhales and counts slowly to five. Then he walks up the driveway, leaves his deck on the porch, and enters into a conversation about him.

"If you don't put your foot down, he's going to walk all over you," Uncle Benji says.

Benji, short for Benjamin, is his mother's brother. They look alike, except Uncle Benji barely has a neck. He works out a lot and always wears shirts that show off his cut arms. In a parallel world, Uncle Benji would share weight tips with Pedro. Instead, Pedro gets a mean mug as a greeting.

"Is this the time you usually get home?" Uncle Benji asks. He knows exactly when Pedro gets home. His uncle has been here more than enough times to figure it out, but he always has to make a comment.

"Mom knows my schedule," Pedro says. He tries his best not to inject any attitude into his answer. This would only cause his uncle to get mad. "I'm going to take a shower."

Uncle Benji blocks his way to the bathroom. "When are you going to start paying bills here? Your mother doesn't even have a decent phone, but somehow you do?"

With each check Pedro gets, he gives money to his mother. But if it were up to his uncle, his whole paycheck would be deposited right into her account. This is not going to end. His uncle wants to get into it, and although Pedro is exhausted, his anger builds. He's so tired of these circular arguments meant only to belittle him. Pedro looks over to his mother, who makes herself way too busy in the kitchen, heating Uncle Benji's food.

She isn't always like this, so catering. When Uncle Benji isn't around, Pedro's mother and he get along as best they can. She doesn't understand Pedro's lifestyle, his clothes, what he does on the phone all day, but at least she doesn't try to forcibly change him. When Uncle Benji appears, it's as if she loses her voice.

"I'm going to bed," Pedro says.

"You haven't even said one word to your mother," Uncle Benji responds. "This isn't a hotel. You don't get to do whatever you want."

Pedro can't keep his mouth shut for much longer. He's going to go off.

"Can you get out of my way so I can go to sleep? I have school tomorrow," Pedro says, intensely staring at him.

"Benji, your dinner is getting cold," his mother says.

After a couple of breaths, his uncle finally steps aside.

Pedro closes his bedroom door. Uncle Benji continues to talk loudly about him.

"He's not going to amount to anything. You're lucky I have time to come over," Uncle Benji says. "I'm going to straighten him out."

Pedro opens his bedroom window. He can climb out and be at La Plaza in forty minutes. He texts the owner and hopes for a quick response.

"God, I hate him so much," Pedro mutters.

To avoid hearing his uncle speak, Pedro practically sticks his whole body out the window, contemplating whether or not to jump. His uncle will stay for a few days, and he'll have to bear it because he has no other choice.

Pedro looks up and notices a weird, unnatural glow in the sky.

"What is that?" Pedro says to himself.

Because he lives in Hollywood, it is not unusual to see a spotlight or two gracing the sky for a movie premiere. This light doesn't have the same radiance he is used to seeing. It covers a large expanse of the sky then stays stagnant, not moving at all. It could be a new promo for a movie or a nightclub. Maybe a rich dick decided to play around with a new toy of some sort.

Pedro tries to capture what he sees with his camera, but it's unable to do justice to what he's witnessing. He waits for a drone to show up. To reveal the glow is just an advertisement for a new yogurt or, even better, a new reality show.

But nothing. *Am I tripping?* Pedro wonders.

A few seconds later, the illumination disappears without a trace. Pedro waits for another to take over the sky or for an announcement. Some sort of explanation.

"I'll force him to work at the garage. Get him a real job."

Pedro ignores his uncle's threats and continues to look at the sky.

CHAPTER 4

Mónica can't stop giggling. She gets this way whenever she's tired. Rafa peels a tangerine and offers her a sliver.

"You have to be quiet," Rafa whispers. "Eat this."

"I want to go. Can we go?" Mónica squirms in her chair like a puppy unable to contain itself. She presses so closely to Rafa on the pew, there's absolutely no gap between them.

They have to wait for mass to end before they're able to eat the free dinner served in the basement of the church. The food is usually cooked by the practitioners. Large serving trays of yuca con chicharrón and home-made pupusas wait for them downstairs. Rafa's stomach growls. The service is almost done. He sneaks a tangerine slice into his mouth, a holdout from today's school lunch. Rafa hands the peel to Mónica. She presses it to her nose and closes her eyes, inhaling the citrusy scent.

"Almost," Rafa says.

Hunger can make a person grow anxious. Mónica is too young to control herself, but Rafa is old enough to be used to this feeling. He's also grown accustomed to hiding it, like most aspects of his life. Don't reveal how hungry you are. Don't divulge any personal facts about yourself. Always exhibit a sense of calm even though, inside, you're panicking about everything.

When the reverend concludes the service, Rafa tries to stop Mónica from running off. One look from Mom, and Mónica sits back down. His parents don't like when they appear too eager.

"How is the new school?" Reverend Pablo asks as he greets Rafa's family.

"Good," Rafa says, shaking the reverend's hand. His parents want to please the reverend who helped him get into the school, so he lies: "I've made friends."

They've been going to this church for as long as he can remember. The church sometimes allows families in need to sleep in the basement. It's not their turn right now, but soon it will be.

When the reverend goes to greet another family, Rafa's father looks over to them and nods. Their signal that they can now go eat.

"C'mon, Rafa!" Mónica pulls at him.

He leads his sister down to the basement, addressing each of the mothers serving the food with a humble nod. One of them hands him a plate. He takes it and Mónica's dish too, to avoid any accidents.

"Sit here," he says. Mónica tears into her meal. "Chew your food, or you're going to choke."

He taps the straw into her juice box and places it

on the side of her plate. His parents sit by another couple. They are deep in conversation, probably about who gets to sleep in the basement after his family.

Rafa spots a girl glancing over to him. Vickie is sixteen, one year younger than him, with hair so long it reaches her waist. They've only spoken a couple of times. Rafa doesn't know much about her except that her parents are very connected to the church. She also has a bunch of older brothers who have their own kids.

When their eyes meet, Rafa politely smiles. She returns his grin and soon walks over holding a glass of juice.

"You forgot this," she says. She has unplucked eyebrows and a birthmark on her cheek the shape of a small heart.

"Thanks," Rafa says.

"I made the pupusas."

He nods with approval. An awkward silence follows the brief exchange. It doesn't stem from any shyness on Rafa's part, although he's always kept to himself. In his last school, and the previous schools before that, he made a couple of friends, but they never really got to know him. The less digging into his life, the better.

Still, Rafa sometimes finds himself wanting to speak to someone closer to his age. He just wishes this interaction wasn't so loaded with expectation. He can feel how their parents are staring at them, adding an immense pressure to connect with Vickie. Arranged marriages may not exist in his culture, but this is something akin to it. But to be close to someone is to be vulnerable, and he won't allow himself that weakness, even in friendship. Maybe more so.

"Do you want another serving?" Vickie asks. Rafa shakes his head. The churchgoers are still staring at them. He gets up to clear his and Mónica's plates, but his sister holds on to it, asking for more.

"I'll get it," Vickie says.

"No, thank you. I'll take care of it." Vickie's face drops a little, like she messed up somehow, and Rafa feels bad. He doesn't want her to misunderstand him or his reactions. He hates this weirdness. He wishes he could just be upfront with her.

Rafa serves another helping of food to Mónica.

"Stay here," he tells his sister. The gawking is too much. He needs a little bit of air. He walks upstairs to the front of the church where kids play, waiting for their parents to finish. Rafa finds a spot away from them, against the church's brick wall. The air is crisp. It won't be too cold for them tonight, and that's something he can hold on to at least.

"There you are," Vickie says, a little breathless. Her smile is slightly crooked. "You didn't get a piece of cake."

She hands him a plate with a generous slice and a plastic fork.

"Our youth group meets on Fridays. Sometimes we go to the movies or just get food," she says. "You should come."

Rafa nods as if he's mulling the idea. He can never afford to go to the movies. Does he tell Vickie the truth, or does he say maybe he'll join them next time?

"I really can't. I have to take care of my sister," he says instead.

"You can bring her!"

Vickie is so excited about this possibility, and Rafa feels a tightness in his chest. He should be honest with her. She likes him, and there's nothing wrong with that. There shouldn't be, at least. It's just that Rafa doesn't feel the same way. In fact, he doesn't feel anything most days, simply anxiety and fear. If anyone would understand, it would be someone attending this church. Still, there are things about him he doesn't want to divulge to anyone.

"I will try," he says. She gleams with hope while Rafa feels like a jerk.

"We asked your parents if you and Mónica wanted to stay with us." Vickie looks down at her colorful Vans. "They didn't think it was a good idea."

Rafa's parents are much too proud to ask for handouts, although here they are eating free dinner at a church. He wishes they would let Mónica stay with Vickie at least for a night, but they think that's asking too much. The only generosity they'll allow is showering twice a week at a volunteer's home.

"There's nothing wrong in asking for help," Vickie says.

Rafa is surprised by her frankness.

"We're doing okay." His tone is even, though he feels a certain way about what she said. "I'm trying to maintain, like everyone else. Like you."

"Maintain?" Vickie says. "What about having fun, or even just talking?"

She wants to save him. Isn't that what this is all about in a way?

"Thank you for this." Rafa shows her the now empty plate. The cake was very sweet. "We're fine, Vickie. I promise you. Just today I had a really deep conversation with this kid at school. We are probably going to talk some more on Friday."

"Oh, good," she says. "What did you talk about?"

"The importance of property and who owns what," Rafa says. "His name is Isaac. I think we are going to be really close friends. I'm sure of it."

Everyone at school thinks Isaac is going to continue their "conversation" during a field trip to the Griffith Observatory on Friday. Rafa has never been there before. What could have been a new place to explore is now turning into his probable death bed. He's going to have to use his fists to get Isaac to back down. It makes him sick when he plays through how a fight at school will hurt his family.

"I'm going to the Griffith Observatory. You ever been?" he asks. Vickie says no. "Isaac is going too. It's going to be fun. Maybe this time we'll talk about the stars."

Vickie gives him a quizzical look. "Sometimes I don't know if you are being serious or if you're joking."

Rafa steps away from the wall they are both leaning on and throws away his empty plate. "I'm very serious."

Smiling, Vickie looks unsure how to respond.

"I'll see you later," he says.

Rafa finds Mónica and walks over to his parents. They are almost done.

"I want to keep playing," Mónica says. She struggles to get away from his grip.

"We need to go. You've played enough. There's school tomorrow, remember?" She eventually stops fighting him. At least Mónica will be so tired, she will sleep right away tonight.

"Rafa, what's that?"

Mónica points up to the sky. A strange glow emanates from above.

"It's probably from Hollywood, like a movie premiere," he says.

"Can we go there?" she asks, her eyes still glued to the sky.

"Maybe later."

They walk toward the bridge, with his parents following close behind. Rafa hears bits and pieces of their conversation. They're figuring out next steps. In a few days, they will be able to sleep in the church basement. There is a mention of Vickie's family. A possible job lead for his father.

If Rafa survives the trip to the observatory, maybe he will bring Mónica to the museum this weekend.

She would like that. A few months ago, he took her to LACMA. Admission was free because of their age. They took in the wild paintings and created their own. Mónica still has her piece, rolled up and held in place with a rubber band.

"The lights, Rafa," Mónica says. "They disappeared."

"Maybe they'll come back tomorrow," he says.

The sky is now dark, as it should be. Rafa plays a round of thumb wrestling with Mónica until the crosswalk turns green.

CHAPTER 5

The school bus smells like bleach. The smell is strong enough to sting Luna's eyes for a few seconds. Her friends have already claimed seats in the back, so she walks toward them.

Luna's overdressed for the observatory, but it felt right to do so. She picked a skirt that had pockets so she could carry her favorite picture of Tasha with her. Most of her pictures of her cousin are in an album on her phone, but one time, Luna decided to make prints. The picture Luna has tucked in her skirt was taken at the Arecibo Observatory in Puerto Rico. Tasha was beaming with excitement at finally visiting. This was before the observatory was demolished because of structural damage and way before Tasha's terminal dance with doctors.

Luna had called out to Tasha, who was paying attention to something on her phone. When Tasha looked up, she stared right into the camera with the widest grin. Luna loved the picture so much she made prints as soon as they got back from the trip. When Tasha became hospitalized, Luna wasn't allowed to visit her. It was at that time when Luna began carrying the photo of Tasha with her. She wanted something to hold in her hands, a reminder of happier times.

"Let me get the window seat," Luna says to Soledad. Soledad complies because she would rather talk to the guy across the way, and Luna knows this. They had already planned the seat exchange. Luna talks to friends in front of her. It's going to be a rowdy bus ride.

Rafa is the last to board. Isaac whistles, and his friends join him. Luna smiles when they do this. It's the only way to push down the growing sadness eager to take over. Rafa sits in front of the bus, close to Mrs. Delgado, the teacher.

He should have stayed home, Luna thinks, *just like me.*

"Don't you feel a little bad for him?" Soledad asks after taking a selfie.

"The person I feel bad for is the bus driver who has to take us there," Luna says just as Pedro stands and makes various loud proclamations before the teacher scolds him. Pedro wears a sweater emblazoned with stars and matching skinny jeans, an obvious and brilliant choice for the observatory.

"I love your sweater," Soledad yells to Pedro.

"Of course you do," Pedro says. "Your basic style is attracted to what it can't have."

Luna laughs while Soledad curses at him. Pedro's always flaunting his wicked tongue. It's a gift to be so quick with the comeback.

When Tasha passed away, Pedro gave Luna a card where he wrote down ten things he loved about her cousin. The list included moments Luna had forgotten, like the time Pedro and Tasha sang a BTS song as part of their choir assignment.

Not many people know, but Pedro asked Tasha out on a date. They went to the Grove and watched a very sweet rom-com. "He's a good kisser," Tasha said afterward. Tasha wanted to go out more, but Pedro never pursued it. She wasn't heartbroken, not deeply anyway. She just wondered if she wasn't interesting enough for him. Soon after that, Tasha started hanging out with Isaac and the others.

Luna couldn't understand how Pedro didn't fall in love with her cousin. His rejection of Tasha most certainly meant a rejection of Luna as well. If Tasha wasn't good enough for him, there's no way Luna would be. So she stays away, allowing only the smallest exchanges between them to materialize.

"I've never been to the observatory," Soledad says.

"I have, with Tasha," Luna says.

This is when Soledad should offer a word or two of condolence. Luna hopes she does.

"Do I have lipstick on my teeth?" Soledad asks. Disappointed, Luna shakes her head.

"I like that color on you," Luna says, feeling like a fraud for letting Soledad off the hook. It's not a bad thing to mention Tasha, but her friends think it's not healthy to keep dwelling on the pain.

The bus finally pulls away from the school, heading up toward Melrose Avenue and eventually making a left on Vermont. Luna peers out the window thinking about Tasha, doing her best to focus only on funny memories. She doesn't want to be sad today. She feels so wound up already.

When Mrs. Delgado isn't looking, Isaac convinces Soledad to exchange seats with him.

"You want one?" He offers Luna a mint, and she takes it. "You didn't want to cut out today with me. I had the day all planned."

"What did you have planned for us?" Luna asks. When the bus makes a sharp turn, she allows herself to lean on him. She needs this attention to drown out the blue wanting to seep in.

"I don't know." Isaac gets flustered. "You know, stuff."

Sometimes she wishes Isaac could stay like this, a little shy and unsure of himself. It's rare that he acts this way.

"Sounds boring," she says.

"You are always breaking my heart, Luna," he says. "When the only thing I want to do is make you smile."

She briefly does. "Corny."

"You like it, though."

"No changing seats," their teacher says. Isaac reluctantly returns to his.

"Oh, well, I tried," Soledad says as she sits by Luna once again. "What did he say?"

"He gave me a mint. I think that means we're engaged," Luna says, giggling.

Luna smells the floral scent of Soledad's perfume. There was a point when everyone in Tasha's circle of friends wore the same scent. Luna no longer does. Smelling it now on Soledad conjures up memories.

For Tasha's fourteenth birthday, she convinced their parents to travel to Puerto Rico. It was their first trip ever to the Caribbean. Tasha's father had family there, so they weren't completely green. They rented this large Airbnb right off the southern coast of the island.

The clear blue of the ocean didn't really attract Tasha, although they spent the first couple of days taking in the waves. The place Tasha wanted to visit was the Arecibo Observatory.

"Wouldn't it be great to be able to touch the stars?" Tasha asked when they were both too riled up to go to sleep. They shared a bed even though the house had more than enough rooms.

"Like the astronauts," Luna said. They kept thinking of what-if possibilities until their own voices carried them into star-filled dreams.

The next day they spritzed each other with their matching perfume before being driven to Arecibo. It was on a Tuesday, which Luna remembers because she noticed how empty the place was. Her uncle purchased VIP tour packages, which meant they were able to get a behind-the-scenes look of the observatory.

"What if we hid somewhere down there?" Tasha

asked as she peered out to the giant telescope. Luna had never seen anything like it. The dish was massive as it rested on a sinkhole. "The world's largest phone," their guide explained to them.

They were escorted inside where the astronomers did their work. A small group of four, all white men, huddled together in discussion. Luna felt this was just a performance for the tourists. A way to pretend they were conducting serious experiments. Tasha waved vigorously at them until they paid attention to her. She had compiled a list of questions to ask, and she was determined. While Tasha bombarded the workers with her inquiries, Luna checked out the multiple screens displaying green lines and making beeping sounds. When no one was looking, Luna pressed her fingertips against one of the monitors. If there were any messages being sent to them right at that moment, she would never know and neither would Tasha.

The rest of the vacation went on its obvious track of food, pool, and beaches, but the only thing Tasha wanted to talk about was the observatory.

"We have arrived!" Pedro says, and Luna is back in the bus as it slowly lumbers up the driveway. Luna's heart tugs at her. This is the place Tasha loved more than anything, and here she is without her. It's not right.

Luna takes a deep breath before getting off. She remembers how Tasha and she smoked a joint before entering. Luna was never a smoker, but Tasha was always pushing her to do wild things. "If your father found out . . ." Luna said, and Tasha just laughed. They were so stoned watching the laser show, like most people probably were. Being loud and obnoxious. What other memories will seep in today?

"Quick! Take a picture of me," Pedro yells at Soledad, and she complies.

If you are here, Tasha, let me know. Send me a signal that you are seeing what I'm seeing, Luna thinks to herself. *Even if it's just to tell me that high school sucks, because it does. Without you, it does.*

CHAPTER 6

Pedro places his hand on his hip, making sure to slightly arch his back. Every few seconds he changes to another pose and then another until Soledad grows tired of being his photographer.

"Thanks, perra," he says and then proceeds to delete most of the outtakes until he's satisfied with one. He posts the pic and watches as his "fans" hit the heart symbol and add those comments.

The edginess he feels doesn't dissipate as it usually does when he works the 'gram. But at least it's Friday, and Friday always means La Plaza once he finishes his late shift at In-N-Out. He just has to get through today.

"Isn't there a merry-go-round near here?" he asks.

Soledad doesn't respond. Instead, she trots off inside to go hang with Isaac and his crew of crap. Pedro follows and looks around at the crowded lobby. Everyone is paired up, and Pedro is left alone. Although he should be used to this, his classmates' actions still irk him. How many years has he known some of them and yet is still considered an outsider?

It's not all their fault. Pedro's always gravitated to the older kids in school, but they've all graduated. There's also this misconception that if you're loud, then you are only good for jokes, for the spectacle, but never for anything more substantial. He knows everyone, but does that really equal a solid connection? Not with this class. You can feel the vibe in the room every time he enters it. No one gives him the attention he needs. Or maybe he craves too much of it.

"If you were a better son, you would do right by her," Uncle Benji said this morning while pouring himself a mugful of their coffee. Pedro watched with contempt as his mother served his uncle a large plate of their breakfast. Uncle Benji taking up all the space at their kitchen table.

Pedro didn't bother eating. The least amount of time he interacts with his uncle, the better. But his uncle was relentless this morning.

"Is that what you're wearing to school? No wonder your mother is upset," he said, and Pedro had to simply allow his uncle to berate him until it was time to go. It's not like Pedro to keep quiet, but this is what he must contend with, being oppressed in his own home. But it doesn't have to be that way at school. The longer people ignore Pedro, the louder he becomes, because why not? Just because his classmates take up so much space doesn't mean Pedro should be unrecognized. No. He will be seen. He will be heard.

"I'm going live and direct from Griffith Observatory, where a white man decided to allow us a tiny access to the sky," Pedro says into his phone.

"No phones, Mr. Morales. Put it away, or I will confiscate it from you. This is your first and only warning," Mrs. Delgado says.

"Miss, if I'm not documenting my life, then is it really happening?" Pedro says. "Who will get to witness this sham of a trip if I'm not here to tell the truth?"

"The phone," she says.

"Okay, miss. I'm going to put it away." Pedro tucks it in his back pocket. His live videos should be considered educational—a sociological experiment for the masses. But no. He has to abide by rules meant to suppress his individuality.

The class listens to their guide, an older white man with gray in his beard.

If only he could sneak away and look for the merry-go-round. Take a series of photos and post them so his uncle can continue to think Pedro is a huge disappointment to the family. How long before his uncle convinces his mother to kick him out for good? How long before he'll have to beg for someone to let him sleep on the floor? Not long.

Why is Pedro even here with these kids and their nice families? This is a joke, like his uncle and his weak threats. Pedro wants to do something, so he does what he normally does when he feels insignificant. He expands.

"Space exploration is just another term for colonialism," Pedro says, loudly. "The only people who can go to space are rich white men."

The guide goes silent. Then, he smiles warmly at Pedro.

"It is definitely not a cheap program, but there is funding to offset the educational stake needed to complete the schooling," the guide says. "Space exploration is open for everyone."

"If you have money," Pedro states.

"White men aren't the only ones who've been out there," Soledad says. "Women, people of color, fool."

Pedro scoffs at her answer.

"This whole thing is just propaganda to get us to invade Mars or Jupiter or whatever planet," he says.

Pedro points to the sky as if he's speaking directly to the galaxies. "But 'conquering space' is code for stripping these planets of their resources to set up condos for themselves, leaving us behind."

Luna chuckles beside him. He can't tell if she's agreeing or just thinks he's ridiculous, like his uncle does. Probably the latter. Pedro looks around. His anger should be directed to his uncle and his sneering, ugly face, but this is where Pedro finds himself instead, in front of kids who consider him a joke.

"Stop buying into what this man is saying. They did it when they landed on Plymouth Rock, and they will do it again in Mars."

"That will be enough, Mr. Morales."

It's not enough. Pedro's just getting started. The fact that they are sitting in this building named after Griffith—who is Griffith if not some white man who wanted to capture the stars for himself? This is as clear to Pedro as the celestial pattern on his sweater. Who are these instructors trying to trick the students into believing they have access to the solar system? No one brown or Black does. He'll be damned if he doesn't let everyone know it.

"This is a hoax. Just listen to the words being used. Conquer. Explore. Plant the American flag and name the planet after yourself," Pedro says.

He walks a bit away from the crowd to give himself more room to project. Some kids egg him on to continue. Others watch in amazement as Pedro continues to interrupt the guide and the teacher. Pedro is on a roll.

"Shut up," Isaac says.

Pedro glares at him. *This football head is trying to shut me up*, he thinks. *No, sir. Not today. Not ever.*

"Who do you think you're talking to? I'm not one of your jockstrap minions following you blindly into a Supreme store so you can cop the latest Yeezys," Pedro says, pointing at Isaac's sneakers. "You're a bunch of sheep."

Isaac steps to Pedro.

"I don't think you want to mess up your cute outfit," Isaac says before lightly pushing him.

"Oh, hell no," Pedro says before launching a punch. He's only able to barely graze Isaac's left check, but it's enough to propel Isaac to retaliate. Luna is pushed against a wall while Isaac and Pedro tussle to the ground.

"You fucking sheep!" Pedro yells.

The class hollers while Mrs. Delgado tries to end the melee.

Another person joins in the fray. It's Rafa, the quiet boy, and this enrages Pedro even more. He doesn't want help from anyone. He just wants to bash Isaac's face and anyone else who gets in his way.

"Enough!"

The guide pulls them apart, sending Pedro to the ground. Pedro breathes heavily while Isaac smirks. At least Pedro was able to land a punch or two. Not enough to draw blood but enough to crease his face.

"You three out!" their teacher yells.

Rafa offers Pedro a hand to help him up. Pedro pushes it away.

"I don't need you," Pedro says angrily.

"Funny, it looks like you did," Rafa says. Unlike Isaac, Rafa has a red bruise right below his eye. The beginnings of a black eye. "I guess I was wrong in thinking that."

"Damn right," he says.

The teacher corrals all three of them to the side. They will be sent to the dean. Not exactly what Pedro intended to happen today, but then again, he did wear his favorite space outfit. Pedro wanted to pick a fight, and he managed to make his wishes come true.

He pulls out his camera and records his teacher telling him how much trouble he's in. Then he shifts the camera to Isaac and then back to him.

"Space exploration is another word for colonization,

and I will not be told different. Not by these heathens. Not by these so-called experts."

He posts the video before Mrs. Delgado takes his phone away.

A teacher's aide is now forced to babysit them while the rest of the class enjoys the field trip. Pedro rolls his eyes at Rafa and then gives Isaac the middle finger.

When Pedro was younger, he was always getting into fights. But it's been a long while since Pedro has had any physical drama. Regret for his actions is starting to creep in, but Pedro jerks it away.

"I hate everybody," he says.

Nearby he can hear Rafa respond with, "Me too."

Rafa doesn't hold his glare, instead he looks away.

The three end up on the bus for the remainder of the trip. Isaac insists he's innocent, and there's a point when the teacher's assistant almost buys in to his sob story. Being the school's star football player has its advantages but Pedro lists the many colorful insults Isaac has called him throughout the years. It felt good to repeat them.

"You are trash, just like your tacky clothes," Pedro says.

"No one cares about you."

And when Isaac said those words, Pedro was reminded of what Uncle Benji told him that very morning. "I don't care about you," his uncle said with such venom. His mother stood silently beside him, never once defending her son.

Pedro starts to laugh and laugh. He can't stop, not even when the teacher's assistant tells him to.

"Quit it, or you're going to get in more trouble," Rafa urges.

But Pedro keeps on until his stomach hurts and a tear rolls down his cheek.

CHAPTER 7

The Griffith Observatory is closed, and what is left behind from the various school visitors is mostly trash. Candy bar wrappers. Empty packs of gum. A forgotten notebook eventually submitted to the lost and found. Fridays are always so busy for the custodians. They usually do a thorough job picking up after the kids. However, this time, one item was overlooked.

Luna's picture of Tasha lies right beside the majestic Ballin wall, underneath the colorful mural of Atlas, the four winds, and the twelve constellations. Before Pedro and Isaac got into a pushing match, Luna held the picture in front of her, trying to remember Tasha from that day in Puerto Rico. She wasn't paying attention to Pedro's antics or the teacher yelling at him. When Luna finally did notice, it was too late. She had only seconds to place the picture back, but she misjudged her pocket. It fell to the floor, and Luna was none the wiser until much later. Somehow the custodians failed to spot it, but it's too late now. Their shift is done. They wave goodbye to the sole security guard as they exit the building.

The security guard patrols the perimeter again, making sure no one tries to sneak in. Ernesto has worked as a guard for five years. The drive to the observatory only takes him fifteen minutes from his City Terrace apartment, where he lives alone. The first time he ever entered the observatory was the day he applied for the job. It was never a place he would consider visiting. Now that he spends most nights there, he's grown to love it. He gets to enjoy it when there are no students, no children screeching about and dirtying the exhibit with sticky fingers. The observatory Ernesto gets to witness is peaceful and relaxing.

Because the facility is located in the south-facing slope of Mount Hollywood, there are several trails ideal for hiking. Ernesto's job is to keep the hikers away from the building, but there is always a straggler or two. Sometimes people want to catch a glimpse of a mountain lion. They bring their telephoto lens in the hope of capturing the beasts in motion. Ernesto chases them away. The mountain lions need their rest too.

The security guard completes the lap around the observatory. He checks his phone and reads a text from the woman he's currently seeing. Her name is Debbie, and she's a real down girl, unlike the other güeras he's dated before. She grew up right in his neighborhood before it became hipster, so she knows what is what. Debbie packed him dinner, which he will enjoy soon.

He runs into the park ranger, and they exchange pleasantries but nothing more. Phil has been working in Griffith Park as long as Ernesto, but for whatever reason, the park ranger considers himself to be his boss. They are both city workers. Ernesto thinks there will soon be a day when he'll have to remind Phil of his place.

"Did you do your rounds already? I thought I heard something by one of the trails," Phil says. "I'll go check it out."

They part, with Ernesto walking back inside the building.

Only a few more hours before dawn breaks open the sky. Phil always enjoys being able to see this happening. It's a beautiful sight to encounter.

The shift in the air is barely noticeable. The park ranger doesn't get wind of it, and neither does the security guard. Both are too engrossed in their lives or their phones or thinking of what they will do after work. But there is a change in the air, in the deep, dark skies. The telescopes will document this.

All around the earth, the Visitors quietly land. They do not approach the atmosphere in what would be considered "typical" spaceships—cold, tin cans depicted in so many science-fiction movies. The vessels the Visitors land on are organic, amorphous, living. They are jellylike and wobbly, almost as if constructed by a child's imagination. The ships' glow is not as intense as it was a few days ago. No one will pick up on its entrance. Inside, each alien is part of the ship itself. The Visitor feeds off the spaceship, and in turn the vessel uses parts of the Visitor to propel itself. The ship is a complete organism.

The vessel lands south of Western Canyon Road, in the densest part of Mount Hollywood. Because of the plasmatic structure, it is easily concealed. The ship dissolves into Mount Hollywood with a minimum amount of noise and nestles right into the growth as if it's always been a part of it.

As the spaceship melds into the earth, the Visitor finally appears. What would the Visitor look like? Like E.T.? The creatures from *Attack the Block*? Or is the Visitor more like a cyborg? Take a closer look at it before it embodies a human form.

The Visitor is gelatinous and viscous. A liquid-looking creature. This is the Visitor's first defense. When encountered, humans will consider it weak and jelly-like, but the Visitor is a sturdier form. Think of walking moss or the Caribbean reef octopus with its ability to change the texture of its skin. The Visitor can expand and contract, and it does so as if it is testing the ability. There are electrical charges flashing throughout the being. And sometimes it becomes a mirror, projecting its surroundings outward, a duplication of the sycamore woodland. Trees and shrubs gravitate toward it like a magnet, searching to make a connection.

Phil is used to strange encounters in the night, and he doesn't want to scare the person or persons. He is gentle in his steps until he stops in his tracks. With his flashlight, Phil directs a small beam of light upward to the

Visitor, who has now expanded, a giant in the growth. Over ten feet tall. The Visitor is an unbelievable monster, a scary and unnatural vision.

The minute the park ranger looks up, his heart rate increases so much so that he clutches his left arm and drops to his knees, the flashlight lost in the dense growth. The park ranger dies with only a small whimper escaping his lips, not enough to alert Ernesto of his impending doom. A heart attack will be used to explain the cause of death, and it's not a lie. Not technically.

The Visitor drifts like the ebb of a tide, gathering branches and leaves within its shape. It moves gently toward the entrance of the observatory and mimics the stairs by converting its form into strict angles. The Visitor is no longer a giant. It is the height of the park ranger it left behind.

Ernesto sits in the main lobby, eating his late dinner. There is a break room for him and the other workers to eat in, but when the place is so empty, he prefers to dine in the lobby with the doors open to allow the night noises to join him. The cold breeze enters the space, and the security guard doesn't mind it at all. There is an October crisp to the air. This is his favorite season. Ernesto thinks about going to L.A. Live to see a movie with Debbie on his day off. Maybe they'll have drinks afterward. There is a Mexican restaurant he can take her to. It's overpriced, but he likes to show off a bit with Debbie, and she enjoys it.

The security guard is immersed in his forkful of rice and beans when the Visitor enters the lobby. "Enters" isn't the right word. It appears to glide across the floors.

The Visitor leaves behind parts of its being as it does this. Its very own specks will stay on the exhibits forever, a type of growth the janitors will foolishly think is a fungus. The custodial crew will use a spray bleach to clean it off, but a residue will stay behind.

A tiny gust of wind alerts the security guard to finally look up. The smell is a mixture of forest and ammonia. So strong, it practically knocks him out.

The Visitor is in its amorphous state, with electric hues of green and blue lights projecting from within like a walking electrical storm. Noiseless. No eyes or a face.

Unlike the park ranger, the security guard's instincts are more street. He grew up ready with fists at the first sign of trouble. It's why Ernesto knew he would make a great security guard. When he first sees this monstrous thing, a thing he can't even formulate with a description in his mind, Ernesto automatically reaches for his gun.

No, that's not true.

Before Ernesto grabs his weapon, he curses. He says "fuck" or "what the fuck." His words are mostly stuck on the tip of his tongue, right at the edge of his teeth.

Ernesto unloads the full cartridge. The bullets just lodge into the walls of the observatory, evidence of a violent attack. Ernesto pushes up against the chair that topples to the tiled floor. The Visitor stops, and Ernesto tries to latch onto something solid, to make sense of this thing. He takes a few steps backward, tripping over the chair. He uses his hands to propel himself away.

He pulls out his phone and presses invisible keys. His eyes are so glued to the hideous creature, he fails to see that he's not calling for help. A string of curses fill the room.

The Visitor is now upon Ernesto. Ernesto shuts his eyes. He prays and prays and prays.

A branch dragged in by the Visitor suddenly juts out from within it like a spear. The branch pierces Ernesto's heart. He slumps down to the ground, his hand still holding the phone.

Mere steps away from this deadly scene is the picture of a vibrant and youthful Tasha still on the observatory floor. The Visitor hovers by the photo before enveloping it into its being. The Visitor's gelatinous form flashes beams of light. Soon scenes project from within the creature: A curious Tasha walks ahead to the observatory. She giggles into Luna's shoulders. A hand touches Tasha's forehead. The number on the digital thermometer reveals a high temperature. A sick Tasha lies in a hospital bed, an oxygen mask over her mouth. A FaceTime call with her cousin is held up to a crying Tasha by a nurse. Tasha is alone in the hospital, surrounded by machines. She dies afraid.

And then seconds pass, and the Visitor is no longer this jellylike aberration. It appears like Tasha, wearing the exact same clothes displayed in the photo. Wavy, pink hair. A disturbing, wide smile on its face.

This new Tasha walks out the front entrance of the Griffith Observatory, leaving behind the security guard, Ernesto, and the park ranger, Phil. The Visitor takes the road down Mount Hollywood and heads to the city.

CHAPTER 8

The bruise on Rafa's eye is now completely purple. His parents were so upset when they saw him after the field trip. "Why?" his father asked, his fury barely contained. He asked Rafa that one question then looked away, not expecting an answer. The looking away was what hurt most of all.

His parents are scheduled to come to school on Monday to speak to the dean. Having to explain this to them was worse than getting sucker punched by Isaac. A fight starts and ends so quickly. Now this incident will carry over to the beginning of the week with Rafa's parents wasting what little money they have to go to the school. His father had secured some hours working early mornings at a bakery, and now he won't be able to do that. This newly found work connection is probably severed because of Rafa's actions.

"Lo siento," Rafa said.

He should have known better before he decided to involve himself. He doesn't even remember what spurred him on. It's not like Pedro is his friend or that he detests Isaac that much. He listened to Pedro's rant in the observatory, and it made sense, the thing about space exploration. Pedro was way more interesting than the guide. Anyway, Rafa didn't think it through, and now the repercussions of his actions are creating a ripple effect. To avoid reminding his family of his mistake, Rafa spent most of Saturday out. He went to the library for a few hours and then tried his luck asking for work in various stores. No one wants to hire an inexperienced high school student, not when men with years of experience are lining up for the few slots available.

"What if you can't see anymore?" Mónica laments when he finally returns.

"I can see enough to know you need to go to sleep," he says. Rafa's father already left for work. It's on him to get Mónica to bed. Only a few more days left in the tent, and then they will be able to get a bit of relief. By then the bruise on his face will be gone and the meeting with the dean forgotten. Rafa hopes, anyway.

"Close your eyes. Tomorrow, I'll take you to the park," he says. Eventually Mónica falls asleep nestled right beside him, her face in the crook of Rafa's elbow. He gently moves her away and steps out of the tent.

There's barely anyone stirring about. He finds a place to use the bathroom, using the small bottle of Purell he carries with him to wash his hands when he's done.

The families who occupy this small space under a highway ramp have known each other for some time.

They share food, water, and most importantly, information. Job leads that might be the lifeline for someone. It's always best to gather together with people you trust.

Across the way, Rafa sees his mother in the corner of the street speaking to a young girl with pink hair he doesn't recognize. Rafa worries when he sees the girl follow his mother, both heading toward him. She's done this before, befriended a runaway for a night, making sure they at least have one warm meal in their stomach before leaving to wherever else their journey might take them. It's an unspoken rule in the community. You take care of the young ones. Rafa quickly goes to the front of their tent, on the defensive as he feels he has to be whenever his mother decides it's time to take care of another stranger.

"Rafa, there's a little bit of soup left," his mother says, indicating for him to fetch it. It's hard to get a good look at the girl. She seems about his age, he thinks. A high schooler for sure. She wears a simple T-shirt and jeans. Nothing out of the ordinary, although it is cold outside. She appears healthy, if dirty. Her sneakers are dusty and her hair full of twigs. The young woman doesn't say a word. She has a strange expression that Rafa can't quite place. It makes him feel uneasy.

He sits on a box crate and offers a seat to the girl while his mother heats up the soup. The girl stares at Rafa, and his whole body is on alert. He doesn't know if this girl will steal from them or cause them harm. He doesn't want to be taken by surprise.

"There are usually a few blankets left for whoever needs it," he says. "Two streets over. You can stay there and move on. No one stays more than a night."

The girl doesn't acknowledge what he says. She doesn't move at all. Not her head, or even her eyebrows. She is so unnervingly still that Rafa finds himself slowly pushing his crate farther away from her.

His mother returns with a very small bowl of soup, just enough to whet the girl's appetite. The girl holds the bowl awkwardly on her lap. Rafa's mother nudges at him to speak, and he tries again.

"Do you need help? The clinic will sometimes take you in, and at least you can be seen by a doctor," he says. "You can probably get fed something way more filling."

The girl doesn't eat the soup. The longer she stares at him, the angrier Rafa gets. If she thinks they can afford to give their food away, she must be on something. That might be the reason she's acting so strange.

The girl moves to touch a group of weeds sticking out from a crack on the sidewalk. The weeds appear to lean toward the girl's hands, as if she's beckoning the growth. There is a slight trace of a smile on the girl's face. A cold shiver runs up Rafa's back.

"Are you going to eat that?" he asks, his tone sharp and clear. He wants her to leave.

His mother shoots him a chastising look. "Rafa goes to Fairfax High School. It's not close, but it's a better school than the high school near here," she says, and he wishes more than anything that his mother didn't offer up any more information to this stranger.

"She doesn't need to know that," Rafa says. Reading his apprehension, his mother stands and carefully takes back the bowl from the girl's hands.

"We need to head inside," Rafa says. "I'll show you where you can sleep."

The girl rises and intensely examines his mother. Rafa abruptly wedges himself in between her and the girl.

"It's not far," he says, pointing the way.

"Here, take this." His mother hands over a thin blanket, not one of their thick ones. "If you need anything, you can ask almost anyone here for help."

The girl takes the blanket but doesn't say thank you. She presses it against her body.

Rafa understands silence. He has lived most of his life surrounded by the loudness of the city. It seems as if the more money you have, the more you can afford to buy quiet. Because he can't have that, he tries not to speak as much. If Rafa can control what comes out of his mouth, then at least he can control something. A whole day can go by when he realizes he hadn't spoken a word.

Somehow this girl's silence seems weighted down by something else. It's hard to explain, and Rafa will spend the next couple of days trying to make sense of this meeting. The uneasiness permeates every second he spends with her. It's more than just the simple "stranger danger." It's something else. He doesn't want the girl to walk behind him, so Rafa slows down until they are both aligned. He pays close attention.

Rafa and the girl finally reach the makeshift sleeping area.

"There you go," he says and turns. The quicker he leaves, the better.

"Why not there?"

The girl finally speaks. Her voice sounds exactly like Rafa's mother, but he doesn't pick up on it. He follows where the girl points with his gaze. There is an empty house across from the tents with a for-sale sign in the front. The light is left on as if to show everyone exactly what they can buy, a cute little cottage of a house, Spanish-style, and completely abandoned.

"Why not there?" It's not even a question, really, the way the girl asks. Again, her voice sounds so familiar to Rafa, yet he can't quite place it. It's the familiarity that confuses him, leading Rafa to dismiss the growing fear.

"We can't just go inside that house," Rafa says, but the girl has already moved across the street. Rafa knows enough, he shouldn't follow. He should turn away because he doesn't want any trouble. And yet he can't stop himself. "Hey, the cops always patrol around here!"

The girl ignores him. She opens the small gate and walks in.

"Don't," Rafa says. The girl continues, opening the unlocked door, probably a mistake made by the agents who appear from time to time to show off the house to potential buyers.

What is compelling Rafa to watch the girl do these things? It's more than curiosity, more than wonder. He should leave this strange girl with the odd voice alone, but he can't. *This is the part of the movie where I'll probably get killed,* he thinks to himself.

"Hey!" He jogs over to the house after making sure no one sees him.

The girl positions herself in the middle of the vast living room. A nice, big space, more than enough room to house a couple of families, not just his.

"You better leave, or they will take you in," Rafa says.

He will only give her a warning, and that will be the end of this interaction. He's done trying to save the lives of others. Just look at how Pedro repaid him, with anger, after he jumped into the fight. But if he could have prevented harm to this girl and did nothing, he wouldn't be able to face his family or his own guilt. It's just not the way he was bought up.

"Why sleep out there when this is empty?" she asks. The peculiar way she says this makes him feel unsteady. The voice is not meant for someone her age.

"I don't know where you come from, but it's not how things are done here," Rafa says. "You've probably already tripped some type of alarm. Why make things worse for yourself? It's not ours."

"It's not ours. It's not ours."

The girl repeats the words again and again in that disturbing voice. She starts to walk toward Rafa.

This is trouble. She's trouble. Nothing good will come

of this. Rafa stumbles out of the house, leaving the strange girl as she continues to utter the words as if casting a spell.

From across the street, Rafa watches the girl still standing in the center of the living room. There is something not quite right with her. He won't be taken in by whatever disturbing fascination this person is exhibiting. Let her hole up in the house by herself. A brown girl is never safe out in the streets. Still, for some reason, Rafa felt he was the one needing protection.

"¿Y la muchacha?" his mother asks when he returns to the tent.

"She's fine," he says. Rafa doesn't want to go into specifics. He doesn't believe his mother would understand.

"Pobre. She's like your age. Too young to be out here alone."

"Go to sleep. Only a couple of hours before we have to get up," Rafa says.

"You sleep soon," she says and kisses the top of his head.

"I will. Soon."

His mother heads inside. Rafa stands guard. He focuses on the house across the street.

CHAPTER 9

Luna can't find it anywhere. The contents of her backpack are spread across the bed. She checked and rechecked her pockets. Dug through every single item she wore the past couple of days, and still nothing.

"Have you seen the picture of Tasha, the one I took of her in Puerto Rico?"

Luna's mother is just about ready to leave for work. She's been on long night shifts, and Luna has barely seen her. This is nothing new, but Luna really needed her mother this weekend. At the very least to help her find the one thing Luna needs to get ready for school.

"No, baby. I haven't," she says. "You sure you didn't put it in the load of wash by mistake?"

Luna checks the laundry room with no luck. The longer she looks for the picture, the more frazzled she becomes, as if she's being punished for not doing enough. A sign from Tasha alerting her that she hasn't visited her at the cemetery, that she's forgotten her. This is far from the truth, but she can't help thinking this is a warning of some sort. She's at fault, and she has to make it right. She has to find the picture.

"It's not here!" Luna says.

"It'll turn up. We have to head out, or we are both going to be late," her mother says.

"No." Her voice cracks. "I need to find it."

Her mother stands behind her and places her arms around Luna's waist. Her first instinct is to pull away. She's still angry at her mother for having to work this weekend. But instead, she lets her mother's cheek press against her back and allows this affectionate act to be as reassuring as it always has been in the past.

"What if it's lost forever?" Luna asks. "It's my favorite picture of hers."

On the back of the picture, Tasha wrote down the date and the words, "We're the stars. I love you, Luna!" followed by a string of hearts. The picture itself she has stored on her phone, but it's not the same thing. Tasha's actual words will be lost forever.

Her mother holds her tight.

"I promise you. You will find your picture," she says. "You will. In the meantime, what can I do to help you feel better?"

Luna wants to give her mother a list of all the things she can do to make her feel anything else but this disappointment. She's kept a growing record of her mother's slights and missed dates. Conversations Luna starts in her head but is too nervous to deliver.

"It's okay." Luna says this more to appease her mom. She wonders if her mother sees the lie.

"I can't wait for my day off. Three glorious days in a row. The hospital has been out of control lately," she says. "You would think it was summertime and everyone was engaging in all kinds of recklessness. It's October, and people are just not taking care of themselves."

Her mother continues to go over the types of run-ins she's had at the hospital, and Luna nods. Her mind races to Griffith Observatory and when she'll be able to get back there.

"I'll make it up to you. This Saturday," her mother says while driving. Luna searches the glove compartment again. "You heard me, baby? We'll visit the cemetery and then have a nice brunch somewhere. Some good cooking!"

"Mm-hmm."

At a red light, her mother squeezes Luna's knees. "I will tear apart the car on Saturday. The picture probably just slipped through the seat somehow."

"Thank you," Luna says.

"Try to have a good day."

Luna nods and closes the car door.

* * *

She flashes her phone in front of Soledad's face during math class. "You've seen this picture?"

"No," Soledad says. "Is that your cousin?"

Luna ignores this answer and turns to Pedro, tapping

him on the shoulder. "Have you seen a hard copy of this picture?"

He briefly looks at the image on Luna's cell phone. "No."

She thinks about showing the image to Rafa but changes her mind, although he looks to her as if expecting her to. Class begins, but Luna doesn't put her phone away. She spends most of the class texting.

* * *

Luna sits at the usual table for lunch. Soledad on one side of her, Isaac joking with his boys beside them. She's counting down the hours to when she can leave and head over to the observatory. Luna hasn't shared this plan with anyone. It's better if she just goes by herself.

"You can just print another copy," Soledad says, exasperated after Luna brings it up again. Luna gets the hint. Her missing photo is not an interesting enough topic for the table.

"Yeah, I can do that," she says and puts her phone away. She feels silly, as if showing how much this means to her is also showing her heart. No one wants to be seen as vulnerable, especially not on a Monday, at the start of the school week, when everyone is ready with their protective armor of invincibility.

The jokes continue. The insults and the jabs. Luna watches the clock's slow rotation. The last bell can't come soon enough.

Rafa walks toward their table. Luna elbows Soledad, who in turn alerts Isaac and the others. If Rafa is deciding that right now is the time to seek revenge for Friday's fight, he's not going to get very far.

"The dean," a boy whispers.

The dean also has his eye on Rafa. Nothing is going to go down—nothing physical anyway. Then why is Rafa walking to them?

"What do you want?" Isaac says, but Rafa is not looking at him or Soledad. He's only looking at Luna.

"The girl on your phone. The picture you lost?" Rafa says. "I spoke to her."

Luna glares at him. Is this some kind of cruel joke, a way of getting back at Isaac by having her involved in some way? She's furious.

"What did you say?" she asks. Soledad smacks her teeth. Isaac stays down but only because of the dean.

"That girl," Rafa points to Luna's phone. "I spoke to her. Saw her a few times this weekend."

"Why would you even say that?" Luna says. She feels like she's breaking.

"You're lucky the dean is right there, or I would have you down on the floor," Isaac says. "Get away from this table before I lay you to waste."

"I just thought you would want to know," Rafa says and heads outside to the courtyard.

"Don't listen to him. He's just trying to get with you," Soledad says.

Luna grabs her stuff and follows him.

"Luna!" Soledad yells.

The faster she walks, the angrier she gets. She finds Rafa sitting on a bench beside Pedro.

"Why would you say that to me?" she says. Pedro looks up from his phone. "Are you messing with me?"

Rafa lets out a long sigh. "I don't know you or her. I just thought you should know."

"Look at the picture. This is who you were talking to?" Luna's hands are shaking. She is so angry.

"It was her. She was wearing the same clothes."

"No! You are lying!"

Everyone in the courtyard turns to them. Luna glances around. They are waiting for her to lose it like she did that one time, the first week back at school after Tasha was gone. But she won't, because she's in control of this, and no matter what Rafa says, the truth will be revealed. This is a mistake. He must have seen someone who looks like her.

"He barely says two words to me in class, and he decides today he's going to tell me this?" Luna speaks to Pedro. Her voice is lowered but not by much.

"Why would he lie about something like that?" Pedro asks. "Seriously? Unless he has some weird kink. Do you have some weird kink?"

"What did she say to you then?" Luna asks.

"She didn't say much."

"You sure you saw this girl?" Pedro asks. "This girl right here?"

Rafa nods. "For the past two days, I've seen her. In those clothes."

"Take me to her then," Luna says. "I want to see her."

"If you're going, then I'm going too," Pedro says. "Whatever weird drama is brewing; I want to see it for myself. I want to see this fake Tasha."

Luna shakes her head. This isn't supposed to be a field trip. "No."

Pedro stands and places a hand on his waist. "First, you don't get to dictate where I walk or with whom. Period," he says. "Second, you don't know him, so I'm going."

"After school then. Meet at the bus stop."

Rafa stalls. He better not be backing out. He's taking her to this person, and then they will all see that it's not Tasha but a poor imitation of her.

"I got detention today," Rafa says.

"What a coincidence," Pedro says. "So do I."

"Whatever. Afterward," Luna says. "You are going to take me to her."

And it was settled.

CHAPTER 10

For detention, Pedro is forced to clean classrooms. He picks up garbage from the floor and wipes the desks down. The dean was smart enough not to place Isaac anywhere near him. He still wants to kick his ass even though it's been a couple of days. It's why he forced himself on this silly mission to find Tasha's evil doppelgänger. He wants Isaac to get wind of it. Let the predictable jock get upset that not only is Rafa spending time with his girl but so is Pedro.

He also doesn't want to go home, so the more time he spends outside, the better. Uncle Benji attended the meeting with the dean this morning instead of his mother. The only thing waiting for him at home is his angry uncle and the excuse to go over what the dean said about him. The funny thing is the dean wasn't even that bad. He spoke on how well Pedro is doing. But his uncle didn't hear one word of it. Too busy catching the negative and adding to the pile he will repeat later.

"Finish up and head next door," the dean says.

Pedro and Rafa grab their rags and the large garbage bin then roll it to the next classroom. While the dean talks on his walkie-talkie, Pedro takes a good, long look at Rafa. His bushy, overgrown hair. The frayed jean jacket. His slender build.

What is up with him? Pedro thinks. *I don't care how cute people think silent types are. I read somewhere that the quiet ones are usually the ones with the loudest minds, and it's true. He's not fooling me.*

"I know what you are trying to do," Pedro says. "Don't even bother."

Rafa sprays cleaning solution across the desk before answering. "Am I wiping the desk wrong? Is there a right way?"

Pedro suppresses a chuckle. Rafa has a type of humor Pedro likes. Quietly bitchy. He doesn't look like the type of person who would string Luna along with this story. It's just too weird, but who knows. People are weird.

"Listen. I don't know you, but I do know Luna. She might not like me for whatever tragic reasons, but I won't stand for her being lied to. Own up to it now before we go meet her."

Rafa stops wiping the desk and lets out a long sigh. "I didn't ask to meet this girl. She just appeared. And I didn't ask to take you two to her. Luna forced me to, and you just invited yourself."

"You got that right."

They continue to clean until Pedro breaks the long silence by punctuating it with a spritz from the cleaning solution. Quiet boys always get to Pedro, probably because he's never been one.

"You know that whole look is played." Pedro says.

"What look?"

"The strong, silent type. It's canceled like patriarchy, gender norms, and space exploration."

"You ever thought maybe your perception of what I'm like is just that?" Rafa says. "A really bad hologram."

"Oh, is this your way of flirting?" Pedro asks, part serious, part not. Pedro likes how Rafa blushes. He also likes how Rafa doesn't look down or away. Instead, he holds his stare, eventually displaying the tiniest hint of a grin.

Huh, Pedro thinks. *The quiet ones always seem to surprise.*

And for the first time in a long while, Pedro finds he's a little nervous of what might be revealed next. He concentrates on wiping the desk and shifts the light tone.

"You don't know the story, so I'm going to tell it. Her cousin Tasha was her everything, and she died from 'rona," Pedro says. "Although Luna comes off like a bitch, she really isn't. Don't play with her emotions, because she's a fragile thing like me."

Rafa tosses a rolled up piece of paper that makes it into the garbage bin.

"Maybe I'm fragile too."

Wow, Pedro thinks. *Look at that.*

"What sign are you? Wait, let me guess. Taurus. No, maybe Scorpio."

Rafa just smiles.

"Definitely Scorpio. Makes sense."

It's one thing to guess his sign but it will take more to fully unravel Rafa. Pedro's noticed how Rafa always walks to school, how he has a younger sister or brother, and how he wears pretty much the same clothes. This in and of itself is not a big deal. A lot of students stick to their personal uniform. Still, Pedro just hasn't invested enough time in Rafa. He might as well hang out with Sad Girl and Quiet Boy on a Monday in search of a ghost.

"Stop hoarding the rags," Pedro says.

"I'm not." Rafa hands him one. Pedro notices his clean fingernails and how underneath his unruly hair, his cheeks are still a little flushed. Eventually, they end up cleaning a desk side by side. They don't speak, but Pedro likes how Rafa's silence doesn't intimidate him. He doesn't feel the need to fill the room with words. Instead, he counts the times Rafa looks his way.

"You two are done. Make sure to get your detention slip signed by your parents," the dean says before his walkie-talkie cackles with noise. Pedro has no intention of getting the form signed. He plans to forge the signature, because the tongue-lashing his uncle will be unleashing on him won't be worth the price of an autograph.

"I need to get something from my locker," he says, and Rafa follows him. Although Pedro's style is loud, his locker is on the minimalist side. He keeps it clean and free of images. Not even a mirror.

Pedro grabs his history book and shoves it into his backpack. Then he takes a Baby Yoda hidden in the back of the locker and tucks it in the front pocket of the bag. The Baby Yoda looks out like it just wants to be saved.

"And yeah, I'm a Star Wars fan," Pedro says. "I'm also a big ears fan."

The two walk toward the bus stop. Luna is there with her usual mask of sadness, now joined by impatience.

"Well?" Luna says. "Where do we have to go?"

Rafa points south, down Fairfax Avenue.

"Fine. Let's take the bus. I see it coming." Luna and Pedro turn in that direction, but Rafa doesn't join them.

"I usually walk," he says.

"Walking? I don't think so," she says.

Rafa shrugs and moves south anyway. Luna looks at Pedro with confusion.

"What's happening?" Luna asks. "Pedro, did I miss something?"

Pedro has never seen Rafa take a bus. He's used to the walking life. Not that many people do it in LA. It's why Pedro usually travels with his board so he can always be on the move, even when he's run out of money on his TAP card. Sadly, his uncle confiscated his skateboard that morning. But Luna is not about that life. She lives in West Adams, and those houses over there are ready for their *Interior Design* debut.

"Wait up, Rafa! We can take the bus," Pedro says, flashing his TAP card. "I got enough to spot you."

Rafa doesn't flinch from embarrassment or act

prideful, which Pedro appreciates. Being poor is a universal thing.

"Okay," Rafa says. "I owe you."

"No, we are even."

The bus arrives, and they are able to find a row of seats together. There are just a couple of kids they don't know riding now. Pedro sits beside a fidgeting Luna. The bus is not going fast enough. Pedro would bet money he doesn't have that Luna would rather drive the bus herself.

"What did she say?" Luna asks Rafa. "And you said she was wearing this?"

Pedro wonders if this ghost scavenger hunt was the best idea. Luna clutches her phone as if Tasha will jump from inside the screen at any moment.

Rafa studies the photo.

"Listen. She was probably just some runaway," Rafa says. "There was something off about her. I can't stop thinking about it."

"Tasha didn't do drugs. She sometimes smoked," Luna says. A handful of beats pass. "She died from the virus."

No one has to say anything more because nearly every single person, from the bus driver to the old lady clutching her bag on her lap to Pedro, had someone close to them die from the virus. Pedro's loss came mostly from the older men who frequented La Plaza, but the virus got young people too.

Pedro pulls out the Baby Yoda and hands it to Luna.

She smiles at the stuffed toy, and this breaks the sadness. Everyone was so into Baby Yoda, but Pedro's Yoda is extra special because it was given to him by a boy he fell in love with.

"This was a gift from Chris, this gorgeous, red-headed Black boy from Hermosa. He wanted to be a rock star or some nonsense," Pedro says. "After treating me to breakfast at Canter's, he pulled out this Baby Yoda and said something like, 'Here, so you can remember that our love really happened.' He was a really good kisser but a little bit too on the nose with the ill-fated drama."

Luna caresses Yoda's big ears. "Did you see him again?"

"Oh, yeah. He turns up once in a while. Does the layup of La Brea, Fairfax, Sunset," Pedro says. "Chris. He was beautiful but lost. Like everyone."

After a few stops, Rafa motions for them to get off on Wilshire, where they take another bus heading east.

Because Luna is getting nervous, so is Pedro. It is as if they are passing their tension back and forth like doing the wave.

"She might not be there," Rafa says. He rubs his hands together then places them in the pockets of his jean jacket. "She was holed up in this empty house."

He's not telling us everything, Pedro thinks.

"Are you afraid of her?" he asks. "Did she do something to you?"

Luna moves closer to Rafa. Pedro feels as if the next

words will plop right there in front of them, creating a horrible crater, dragging them all down.

"No, not afraid, just uncomfortable." Rafa looks at the dirty floor of the bus, and the three stay silent for the rest of the ride until he rings the bell. They disembark, with Rafa leading the way. They walk past a long row of tents, and Rafa greets people with a nod or a quick hello.

He lives here, Pedro thinks. The thought is absolute to him. This is where Rafa sleeps, among these people. With that knowledge, he sees Rafa in yet another light. Another complicated layer.

"She's there." Rafa says, his voice breathless.

"Where?" Luna grabs hold of Pedro's arm. Pedro places his hand over hers to calm her, but this only makes her hold tighter.

Across from the tents sits a girl in front of a house up for sale. She sits on the porch as if she lives there. The girl is dressed exactly like Tasha in the photo. Identical. There is an eeriness to this, and Pedro finally catches on to why Rafa is apprehensive.

"Oh my god. Tasha." Luna whispers these words while a fear increasingly grows within Pedro.

The girl sits with perfect posture. Her hands on her knees. She doesn't move.

"Wait," Pedro says, but Luna is no longer by him. She runs across the street, dodging cars, toward this girl. She calls out her name.

"Tasha! Tasha!"

"Shit," Pedro says. "Don't just stand there, Rafa. We got to go."

He runs after Luna.

"Tasha," Luna says, on the verge of tears. "You are here."

The girl has an uncomfortable smile on her face, a grin stretching across her lips. Pedro has seen that look before sometimes on the faces of the people he serves at In-N-Out. Doll-like empty grins with no substance behind them. A shiver runs up his spine. Pedro wants to walk away from this girl, this fake Tasha, but he can't leave Luna. She doesn't see what is right in front of her. Doesn't see what Rafa has been trying to warn them of ever since they got on the bus.

"That's not Tasha," Pedro says. "Luna, that's not Tasha. I don't know who that is."

But Luna doesn't listen.

CHAPTER 11

Rafa watches Luna follow the girl inside the empty house. This will not end well. He should leave Pedro and Luna to deal with this on their own. He did what they asked him to do. He owes them nothing.

"C'mon!" Pedro turns to Rafa once more before running after Luna.

"No thanks. The cops are around here all the time," he yells, but it's too late. Pedro and Luna are inside.

What the hell do I do? Rafa thinks. There is something off with the girl. Why didn't he just tell them that instead of holding back his words?

He runs across the street to the front door, but it is locked. He knocks but not too loud so as not to draw attention. Any minute now cops will be called. They need to get out of there.

"Pedro, open the door!"

A couple walking by eyes him with suspicion. The door won't budge. Rafa races to the back of the house to try to find another way in. He's caught off guard by how overrun with growth the backyard is. The grass hasn't been mowed in what seems like months, but he's almost sure this wasn't the case a couple of days ago. He pushes aside the unruly landscape to reach the door.

Why does this feel like a trap?

He turns around to face the backyard, and the growth appears to expand. Something rustles within it, movement from a corner, but Rafa can't see what it is. It must be a cat, he thinks. What else could it be?

He opens the door, and an acidic stench hits him so strongly, his eyes immediately water. The smell irritates his throat, constricting his lungs. It takes a few seconds for his eyes to adjust to the darkness. When it does, Rafa notices the kitchen is more like a forest. Strange plants cover the ceiling and the floor. Drops of dew fall on his face, and a heavy humidity blankets his skin.

What is this?

People's voices sound muffled and far away. Rafa doesn't want to enter, but they are both in there somewhere, in this disturbing place that makes no sense.

"Luna!" Rafa yells. "Pedro!"

He pulls out a bandana tucked in his pocket, a habit cultivated in the virus days, and wraps it around his mouth and nose. Every step he takes is carefully placed on what feels like shifting ground. He uses the sleeve of his jean jacket to push away the dangling mosslike plants. It's so dark, but he doesn't want to waste time looking for a light switch, not when the surfaces are completely covered in green.

"Pedro!" he yells again.

Rafa enters a hallway that leads to the living room. His heart is pounding. It takes him minutes, but the minutes feel like hours. Things brush against his jacket and his hair. Things he doesn't want to think too much about. He must focus on finding Luna and Pedro.

"Is it really you, Tasha?"

Luna's voice emerges from within the denseness. Although muted, Rafa is able to anchor on to it. He walks toward them, taking shallow breathes to avoid coughing.

The strange girl stands in the center of this unruly foliage. Pedro holds Luna's hand, the only thing stopping her from rushing toward the fake Tasha. The windows are concealed with moss and vines. Rafa has a strange sensation that the room is beating, as if the walls enlarge and contract ever so slightly.

"Let's go outside where it's safe," Pedro pleads. He tugs at Luna.

"Tasha?" Luna asks, her voice breaking. "Talk to me, and I'll know."

The smile is not as wide, but the girl's expression is still distorted.

"Remember? I took this picture of you." Luna shows the picture stored on her phone of Tasha in Puerto Rico. The light from the phone exposes the plants inching toward Luna, but Rafa fails to see this. "Do you remember?"

The girl doesn't look at the screen. She only looks at

Luna, and the smile slowly dissolves, replaced with a dead profile.

"Do you remember?" The girl repeats Luna's words. Her voice has changed from when Rafa first met her. She is mimicking Luna, her exact cadence—right down to how Luna ends her sentences in a higher pitch. Rafa's legs begin to tremble.

"I remember being alone in the hospital," the girl says, still in Luna's voice. "And the pain. I was afraid."

Luna openly weeps. The foliage draws nearer to her ankles, slowly creeping up her legs.

"Oh my god," Pedro says.

"We need to go," Rafa whispers to him. "Now."

"I remember the pain," the girl repeats. "And the promise. Did you keep your promise?"

Luna is inconsolable.

"I didn't want to leave you there. I'm so sorry," she cries. Luna reaches out to the fake Tasha.

The girl seems to regard Luna's hand. Luna's fingers lightly brush against the girl's skin. There is a rustling above Rafa's head. He looks up, and the dangling vines wrap themselves around Luna's waist. Strange flora lifts her up toward the ceiling, welcoming her into the unnatural growth. Pedro screams.

"Let her go!" Rafa yells at the girl while tearing at the plants. Prickly thorns embed in his skin. Tiny drops of blood emerge. He grabs hold of Luna's body and yanks as hard as he can. The vines have too strong of a hold.

"He said let her go, you fucking bitch!" Pedro turns to help Rafa.

The fake Tasha blankly looks at the three.

"I remember," she repeats. "The pain."

"What the fuck did you do to her!" Pedro yells. "What the hell are you?"

"I remember."

"Let her go!" Rafa shouts.

Luna drops down to the center of the room. Her eyes are closed, but she's breathing. Rafa won't look at this fake Tasha, because the girl is evil, and they need to run. Rafa grabs an unconscious Luna and lifts her over his shoulder. With his other hand, he pulls at Pedro, who continues to curse at the strange girl. Her smile is the same one in the picture. The exact same one.

Pedro and Rafa run out of the door and through the gate of the small house. They cross the street, scared out of their minds.

"What the fuck was that?" Pedro screams.

"I don't know," Rafa says, panting. "Jesus, I don't know."

Rafa leads them toward the nearby park. He won't take them to the tents. He can't afford to endanger his family. The park is not too far. It's dark enough that they will hopefully be ignored.

"Is she following us?" Rafa asks.

"You think I'm looking back?"

The three enter the park, with Rafa trying to find the right spot to lay Luna down. He spots a tree and is gentle with her as he places her beneath it. Pedro pulls out a bottle of water from his backpack and hands it to Rafa. He tilts Luna's face and presses the bottle to her lips.

"Luna, wake up," he says.

Those in the park are stirring. Someone else has entered. Rafa can smell the acidity in the air. The hint of it.

"Rafa," Pedro says with urgency. He must smell it too.

"She's not waking up," Rafa says. "What do we do?"

The girl walks toward them. Rafa doesn't need to see this. He can feel it. Pedro grabs the bottle and splashes water on Luna's face.

"Wake the fuck up!" Pedro yells.

Luna jerks up, coughing and spitting out water. Her eyes are still closed, but she starts to lash out at Pedro and Rafa. She screams and kicks while the two boys try their best to calm her down.

"Hey! Hey! What do you two think you're doing?" a man from the park yells at them. "You can't come up in here with this foolishness. Not in my park."

"Luna, it's us. Pedro and Rafa," he pleads. "We left the house. Open your eyes, please!"

The man gets closer. On the far end of the park, the girl who looks like Tasha also edges nearer.

When Luna finally awakens, she looks around frantically as if confused about where she is. Her breath is rapid. She tries to get up, but her legs are not sturdy enough.

"She's coming," Pedro says. "We have to get out of here."

"What's going on?" The man from the park is upon them, and he's angry. Rafa rises and presses his hands up, palms forward, to show the man he is free of any wrongdoing.

"She wasn't feeling well. But she's better now."

"You can't be doing that here. You need to go find somewhere else to do that. Not here."

Pedro helps Luna stand. Even now after what happened, her eyes search for the fake Tasha.

The girl is being stopped by a couple who live in the park.

Something moves underneath Rafa's shoes. The ground is shifting, like in the house.

"Do you feel that?" Pedro asks.

Someone yells, "Earthquake!" Violent tremors begin. The fake Tasha is in the center of the park now. The couple who confronted her lay still on the ground. They are not moving, but everyone and everything around them is.

Rafa urges Pedro and Luna to keep going. The boys hoist Luna up on their shoulders. The swirl of people slows them down, but they are able to keep pressing, heading north, away from the park and the girl.

"Oh my god," Luna says. She leans on Pedro, her eyes still glued to this thing that looks like her cousin. The girl continues to walk toward them.

It's impossible to move in a steady line, what with the earth shaking, but they must flee.

CHAPTER 12

Items fall from atop buildings. Cars pull over to the side.

"Is this the big one?" a man yells from his car.

The two boys hold Luna up as they push against the swarm of people running in all directions. Luna tries to shake off the sluggish sensation. It is as if a gauzy film has been placed on her brain.

"How?" she asks. "It was Tasha. It doesn't make sense."

"Let's stop here." Rafa directs them toward an awning. It's not secure, but it's better than trying to navigate this unrelenting caravan of scared people racing here and there. They need a moment to figure out where to go next.

And just as it began, the shaking stops. Luna leans against the building, although nothing feels secure.

"Were we drugged?" Pedro asks. "Did we inhale something when we entered the house?"

"I have to go," Rafa says.

"Wait a minute? What do you mean?" Pedro says.

"We can't leave now, not after what we just saw. We need to process this. Set a game plan. Do something."

"She knows where my family lives," he says. "I have to protect them."

"No. We have to go to the police," Luna says. There is no way they can manage this on their own.

Rafa is adamant. "No."

Luna bristles with anger. "We need to tell someone."

Pedro agrees with Rafa. "What are you going to say? You might as well tell your story to the 'gram because we'll get a better reception than the LAPD. Literally. Think about it for a second."

Luna slaps her hand against her thigh. "We can't just ignore it and pretend it didn't happen."

"Us nobodies trespassed into an abandoned house where what, exactly, happened?" Pedro says. "This evil demon ghost girl managed to literally get a freaking ceiling to almost eat you."

Luna covers her face in shock.

"She looked just like Tasha. How is that possible?" she asks. "There has to be an explanation. There just has to be."

"Forget about it. That's what I'm doing," Rafa says with conviction. "I need to take care of my family."

Pedro tries to stop him, but Rafa is determined.

"I can't forget about it!" Luna yells, catching up to both of them. "We saw her. She was right in front of us. And that house. It happened! Let's get help."

"The cops will do absolutely nothing. I can't afford to

put myself out there, not when my family is in danger. Leave me alone."

Luna and Pedro watch as Rafa crosses the street, leaving them behind.

"He's right," Pedro says. "It won't make a difference. No one will believe us."

"What do we do? Nothing? I can't."

Pedro wipes the sweat from his face with the back of his hand. "She looked just like Tasha. Like she didn't even age or nothing."

He slides down to the dirty sidewalk. Luna joins him.

"I'm scared, Pedro," Luna says. "I'm really scared."

Luna had always imagined what it would be like to see Tasha again, even in her dreams. But Tasha never appeared before her. The recurring dream she has always stops right before she can see whether or not Tasha is in the hospital bed. The idea of Tasha roaming the earth is too much. An unsettled ghost. Is that even possible? Luna doesn't believe in ghosts or spirits or any of those things. She knows Tasha died two years ago. How would she explain this to the police or even to her mother?

"We can't tell anyone," Luna says, allowing the decision to finally hit home.

"At least we were there."

"What does that matter? I can look at you in class tomorrow and we won't say a word, but we'll know?" Luna says in anger. "Who cares?"

"It's better than nothing," Pedro says. "We know the truth, or parts of it anyway. We can shelve it, put it away.

Chalk it up to another messed up Monday in Los Angeles where three kids saw visions."

The two go quiet, fall deep in their thoughts. The streets soon settle down. Luna eventually calls a car to take her home. Pedro waits with her until she is safely inside.

"It wasn't a hallucination," she says. "It was Tasha or something close."

"Here." Before Pedro closes the car door, he airdrops his phone number to her. "Text me when you get home, please."

She agrees to and the car pulls away.

✳ ✳ ✳

When the driver parks in front of her house, Luna hesitates before exiting the car. She does a quick scan of both sides of the street then pulls out her keys and holds them out like a weapon.

She walks quickly to the front of her house and enters. Turns on all the lights and texts her mother to let her know she's home. Her mother responds with a smiley face.

When do you get off work?

Luna rarely asks this of her mom. She doesn't want to alarm her, but Luna's also holding a kitchen knife, just in case.

The usual. I'll see you soon.

She sends Pedro a text that she's safe at home and then tests the alarm, making sure it will go off if anyone tries to come inside. She draws the curtains. When the home is as secure as she can make it, Luna finally sits on her bed. She is sweaty and exhausted, with scratches covering her arms and legs.

With the door to the bathroom wide open and her phone right by her, Luna enters the tub for a quick shower. Her fingers trace the scratches. She goes over the events.

The mirror to the bathroom fogs over, and she swipes it clean to see herself.

"It happened," Luna says to her reflection. "I saw Tasha. This girl spoke, and I was lifted up by branches, and then everything went dark."

She sinks to the edge of the tub and cries.

Luna left the door to her bedroom open so that she can hear any unusual noises. Her stomach growls, but she refuses to move. She takes her phone out and stares at the picture of Tasha.

After Tasha died, coldness formed between Tasha's parents, Johnny and Rosa, and her family. Nothing in particular happened. They just sort of stopped communicating. Eventually her Uncle Johnny and Aunt Rosa separated, with her uncle moving to Irvine.

Luna felt the loss. They always spent time together. There were BBQs and game nights, sleepovers and family dinners. Each year they would plan a vacation. It was how they ended up in Puerto Rico to visit the Arecibo Observatory. They were a family, and when Tasha left, their union dissolved. It was as if Tasha was their only link, and once she was no longer part of the equation, the relationship no longer mattered.

It's late, but she calls anyway. Luna thinks she should reach out to him even though it's been months since they last spoke, not counting the courtesy calls during birthdays.

The phone rings three times before he answers it.

"Luna! How are you?"

Tasha's father, Johnny, has a deep baritone voice. Tasha always said his voice sounded like bass playing in a song. Johnny joined the force straight out of college. After Tasha's death, he quit and now works as a security consultant.

"I'm fine," Luna says. She chooses her words carefully, unsure exactly what this phone call is really about.

"How's your mom? And school?"

She answers the prerequisite questions as best she can. Luna is not sure how to broach the subject.

"So, is there something you want to talk about?" Uncle Johnny asks after the inevitable lull in the conversation.

"I was wondering . . ." Luna says. How to even begin? What could Luna possibly say to him that would make sense?

"I know, I know," Uncle Johnny says. "I miss her too. I miss her every day."

The wound opens, an accumulation of anguish slowly trickling out.

"Have you seen her?" Luna asks, and she immediately regrets it. What will he think of her?

There is a long pause.

"I see her in the most unexpected places. Sometimes there will be a flash of color, usually a soft pink, and I will think it's her running past me," he says.

Then, another moment of silence.

"When I look up to the stars, I'm reminded of how she loved to study them. Forcing us to travel to all those observatories." He chuckles at the thought. "Tasha was a funny baby."

Uncle Johnny's lost in his memories. Luna cradles the phone tightly.

"But you haven't seen her, not even in your dreams?" she asks.

"No. Not even in my dreams. Has she been visiting you? Maybe she wants to tell you something. Or maybe it's just you trying to send a message to another part of yourself."

"I don't know what she wants," Luna says. "What if I get the message wrong? If it's not a warning but something else. What if I failed her somehow?"

"Have you spoken to your mom about this? I think you should," he says. "This time of year is always so hard. It is for me, and I'm sure it is for you. Just remember that Tasha loved you, and her love was the best thing she gave to each of us."

They end the call with the usual vows of keeping in touch and getting together. Love to Luna's mother and have her call me, and the like. It wasn't exactly what Luna wanted to say to her uncle. She wanted to tell him that she saw a version of Tasha, an inverted copy of her cousin that defied logic.

"The promise," Luna says.

It was the last conversation they had before Tasha couldn't take any more calls. Uprisings against police brutality were forming all over the city, escalating in her community when a young Latinx boy was shot by sheriffs. Tasha was adamant about speaking out, but her sickness kept her watching the action from a hospital bed.

"You have to promise me you'll join the protests," Tasha asked. "I don't care what my father says. They shot him. He was our age."

Luna promised she would join the protests. Make signs, even. But she never did. Instead, she hung out with Isaac and buried her sorrow. Now her remorse is tenfold.

"I'm so sorry," she says, crying until exhaustion takes over.

CHAPTER 13

Entering the tent, Rafa startles his parents, who were quietly speaking to each other in the dark. For the most part, the area had settled down from the earthquakes, but they are worried about aftershocks. Mónica is barely able to keep her eyes open. She's so tired, but her parents won't allow her to sleep. They must move to a secure place.

"¿Dónde estabas?" his mother asks.

"Lo siento. I was taking care of something," Rafa says. He quickly helps them gather their things. There is no point in wasting words on excuses.

"Where can we go?" Rafa asks his father, who brusquely directs him to finish collapsing the tent.

"La familia Gonzalez," he says. "Apúrense."

Rafa hoists a couple of bags and lifts Mónica. She rests her head on his shoulder, instantly falling asleep.

"¿Qué te pasa, Rafa?" his mother asks. "You were supposed to be here, helping us, not out there."

I am failing my family, Rafa thinks. He doesn't know what to say to help comfort them. From their point of view, he has been jeopardizing everything they have worked hard to give him. He's been getting into fights and staying out late. This isn't what they expect from him.

He apologizes once more, and they continue in silence. When they reach the Gonzalez house, the head of the family quickly ushers them in.

"Please, make yourself at home," Mr. Gonzalez says, directing them to store their belongings in an alcove off the side of the living room. The Gonzalez family has a small home, but the dining room has already been converted into a makeshift bedroom. Rafa is asked to lay a snoring Mónica on the inflatable bed. The adults head to the kitchen, recounting the earthquake again.

Rafa rubs his eyes. The night feels endless. He will never be able to shake the vision of the girl and the way the house seemed to breathe.

"Impossible," he says.

"Hey." Vickie startles him to the point that Rafa almost spills the glass of water he was meant to drink. Vickie wears jeans and a T-shirt. Her hair is up in a high bun.

"Are you okay?" she asks. "Can you believe I didn't feel the earthquake?"

Rafa nods. She grabs items from the refrigerator to make a sandwich. She motions to ask if he wants something to eat, and because he is a guest, he says yes, though he doesn't have much of an appetite. Vickie leads him to a breakfast nook and pours two large glasses of orange juice.

"I heard my parents talking earlier, something about you being in a fight?" she says. "You don't like Fairfax?"

It seems so long ago, the thing with Isaac. Silly to think this is the topic of conversation in the Gonzalez family. Vickie serves him a sandwich then takes a small bite from hers. She has a very sweet smile, the complete opposite of the monster he saw earlier. A real, genuine grin full of warmth.

"Have you been noticing anything different?"

Vickie laughs. "Like an earthquake? I told you I didn't feel it."

"No, other things. Weird things."

Vickie thinks, scrunching her nose a bit. "Well . . . Some people believe earthquakes are predictions of what's to come, like an alarm alerting everyone our time is limited," she says. "My parents believe most people are lost and this is God reminding us to get back on track."

"So, you think this is the beginning then?" he asks.

"Maybe," she says. Vickie places her sandwich down on the plate. "Can I ask you something personal?"

He waits for her to continue.

"Are you feeling lost, Rafa?"

Rafa is not sure how to answer. He closes his eyes for a second.

"I don't know what I feel. Nothing makes sense." What he saw will be lodged deep in his mind forever. He can't share it with anyone. The sooner he forgets about it and concentrates on his reality, the better.

"Praying helps. Do you want to pray right now?" Vickie asks. "Maybe you won't feel so lost."

Vickie leads Rafa into a short prayer, and when it ends, she recites another one. Rafa doesn't say the prayers out loud, but his lips move along to them. When she's done, Vickie returns to eating her meal.

He's grateful for this kindness even if he's still struggling. At least for now, Rafa is in a house with a roof over his head. His family is safe. Mónica is asleep mere steps from him. Tomorrow he will go back to school and forget what happened. The fake Tasha will not be his problem. Pedro and Luna will have to find someone else to decipher this horror. He can't keep messing up. The stakes are too high.

"Thanks, Vickie," he says.

"You're welcome, Rafa."

He eats his sandwich and takes a sip of orange juice.

CHAPTER 14

Pedro doesn't bother looking up when the bus drives past the stop nearest to his home. He ignores the messages left by both his uncle and mother, asking where he is. His mind clamors with confusion. There is no way Pedro would be able to process this at home while they yell at him. Instead, Pedro decides to go live.

"I'm checking in with you. What's going on? Anything weird besides the earthquake?" He scrolls through the Instagram comments on his live, mostly of people stating whether they felt the earthquake or not. Jokes about the aftershocks and how it's the end of the world and we need a new TikTok challenge to commemorate it.

"Something is definitely wrong," he says. His eyes jot about in fear. *"I'll share more later when I can, but be safe out there. Keep inside, and don't talk to strangers."*

He tries to keep things light, but it's hard to be fake. *"I know I look like a mess, but listen to your favorite perra, please stay inside. Laters."*

Pedro is sure Uncle Benji will see the live post. He

will share it with Pedro's mother, and that will be enough to let them know he is fine, although he will still get in trouble. It doesn't matter. He already got Melissa to cover his shift at In-N-Out. Pedro won't be going home tonight. He needs to talk to someone who sees him.

He checks online for any other news of what happened in the park, but there's only earthquake coverage and nothing more. He gets up from his seat and tries calling La Plaza again. The bar is closed on Mondays, but sometimes the owner will open it to a small, select group for drinks. Pedro's calls go unanswered. He prays there is someone at the bar, or this bus ride will be a complete bust.

"Be careful," the driver says as Pedro gets off. He closes the door before Pedro can thank him.

The stop is a short block away from La Plaza on La Brea. At this hour, this stretch of the avenue is desolate, with most people venturing to Pink's Hot Dog stand farther south. You wouldn't even notice La Plaza because it is so unassuming. The very simple, square structure nestled between two buildings looks out of place and rundown, with its wooden sign in need of a paint job.

"Hello!" Pedro knocks on the front entrance, but no one answers. "It's me, Pedro."

The owner of La Plaza is this half-Mexican, half-Black legend who goes by the name of Mr. Reiña. Mr. Reiña gives the best hugs in Los Angeles. You leave feeling whole again even when everything around you is breaking down. It's exactly what Pedro needs right now.

Pedro walks to the back of La Plaza. On the side of

the club is an entrance where workers sometimes congregate to smoke. The door is also locked, but this time Pedro uses the secret knock only given to a handful of Mr. Reiña's patrons.

"Ya voy!" someone yells from inside. Pedro quickly tries to make himself look presentable. A sound of a bolt, and the door opens.

"The shakes got you too?" Mr. Reiña asks before letting him in. "Come on. You know the drill."

"Thank you," Pedro says before he heads to the bathroom. He washes his face and neck, does a thorough job of cleaning himself up. When he's done, Pedro wonders if he will tell Mr. Reiña.

What do I even say?

In the empty club, Mr. Reiña sits on a barstool watching the news while his partner, Luis, tends bar.

"Do you want something to drink?" Luis asks.

"Serve him chamomile tea," Mr. Reiña says. "I'll take some too. Pedro, say hello to Daniel."

Daniel lounges on a sofa tucked in the corner of the club. He nods hello and goes back to staring at his phone. Though Pedro has seen Daniel at Plaza a couple of times before, he doesn't know him that well. Pedro pulls out a barstool and sits by Mr. Reiña, waiting for the mug full of hot chamomile to be placed in front of him to begin.

"I think I saw a ghost," Pedro says.

"Well, this is going to be interesting," Luis says while lowering the volume to the television.

"Not sure if it was technically a ghost. She seemed real." Pedro remembers she definitely didn't smell like Tasha, who always wore floral perfume. The fake Tasha had a strong scent of ammonia. It was enough to make his eyes water.

"You sure it wasn't just an ex?" Daniel asks jokingly. He still doesn't look away from his phone.

Pedro sighs. He sounds ridiculous. But what else is new? If he doesn't voice what happened, it will only stay between him, Rafa, and Luna. Even if they don't believe him, at least he can bring it out into the open and try to untangle the mess.

"Tasha's been dead for two years, but today I saw her." Pedro picks at the side of his face. "It looked just like her. It was unreal." To calm his quivering voice, he takes a sip from his tea.

"What did this ghost say to you?" Mr. Reiña asks.

"She kept saying she remembered the pain," Pedro says, shaking his head. "Why can't my spectral encounters be joyful?"

"Then it wouldn't be a ghost," Luis says. "It would just be a regular night at La Plaza. Are you okay?"

Pedro takes another sip and places the mug down on the counter.

"Yes. I don't know. Probably not. I'm a mess. I'll just add this to the long list of things to discuss with my future therapist."

He can't ignore how the fake Tasha sounded. Unnatural. And how the plants lifted Luna up to the ceiling. He can't tell them that part of the story yet. It's so hard to explain.

"Then the earthquake happened, and we ran away," Pedro says. "It was her and not her, if that makes sense."

Pedro looks away from Mr. Reiña's concerned expression. Instead, he concentrates on a painting of Juan Gabriel hanging above the bar. Mr. Reiña stands and presses the button to turn on the music system. Sade plays softly in the speakers.

"I've never had the honor of a ghostly visitor. It's not to say it can't happen," Mr. Reiña says as he picks a piece of paper from off the floor. "Perhaps this earthquake is uncovering things. Holy and unholy."

"I'm scared it's not a good sign. I had a run-in with a coyote the other day, and then I got into a fight. With a boy, not the coyote," Pedro explains. "Don't bad things come in three?"

Luis nods. "They sure do."

Pedro tries calculating if Luna being dragged up to the plants is the third thing or if it's the earthquake. Or perhaps none of those things are true. The third thing is yet to drop, an unforeseeable doom he's totally not prepared for.

Daniel gets up from the sofa and starts to sway to the music. "What if she comes back?" he asks dreamily as if he's on the verge of sleep. Pedro can see Daniel dancing from the mirror behind the bar.

"How do I protect myself from seeing her again? Is there mace spray for ghosts?" Pedro asks.

"What was your relationship with her?" Mr. Reiña asks. "Did it end well?"

"We were friends. She tried to be more than friends, and it didn't work out," he says. "I don't think she came back for that. Do you?"

"Wouldn't you come back for vengeance?" Luis says. He dyed his hair blond, but the dark roots are starting to show. "It would probably be the sole reason for me to come back. Get back at all them bitches."

A fake Tasha out for revenge. He needs a weapon, sage, something to protect himself.

"I'm not ready," Pedro says.

"Always be ready," Mr. Reiña says. "So you don't have to *get* ready."

"Besides, this ghost may be your salvation," Daniel says as he slowly spins around.

Pedro doesn't believe for one second the fake Tasha is his salvation, not after what he saw her do. Nothing makes sense, but at least he can hold on to this moment: watching Daniel dance and Mr. Reiña clean up the bar. Here he feels safe, and the strange occurrences he witnessed earlier in the day can wait to be deciphered.

His phone buzzes, and it is his mother reaching out to him. Mr. Reiña raises his eyebrow.

I'm staying at a friend's house tonight. Everything is fine, Mama. I'll be in school tomorrow.

Cuídate, mijo, his mother texts back. His uncle is most likely not by her so she feels brave enough to text him.

She's trapped in the house just as much as Pedro is. At least he has an out, temporary as it is.

"School tomorrow," Mr. Reiña reminds him. Because there are plenty of times when Pedro finds himself in need of a place to crash, he has a set of clothes at La Plaza. He would never repeat an outfit. Pedro might not feel good on the inside, but at least he always looks good.

Before Mr. Reiña walks him to the guest room, he gives Pedro a tight hug, and Pedro melts into the welcoming embrace. He needed it and is thankful to Mr. Reiña and La Plaza for always saving him.

The guest room has plants covering every available nook. Pedro has slept there countless times before, but tonight is the first time he hesitates.

"I should sleep on the couch," he says.

"Daniel has the couch. Be happy you got the jungle," Mr. Reiña says. "My green babies will help you sleep. Don't worry, the sun will bless you tomorrow."

Not wanting to sound ungrateful, Pedro thanks Mr. Reiña for his generosity.

Later that night, when Mr. Reiña and Luis are asleep in their room, Pedro restlessly tosses and turns. He covers his body with the sheet to avoid looking at the plants. Eventually he dozes off, but Tasha's distorted voice haunts his dreams.

CHAPTER 15

When Pedro enters the classroom, he immediately seeks Rafa and Luna. Rafa keeps his head down. Luna glances at him for a brief second and then looks away.

"Y'all can't be serious," Pedro says. "We're not entering Tuesday with you both ghosting me, not if I can help it."

He didn't sleep much, but from what he can plainly see, neither did Luna or Rafa. They look like crap just as much as he does. On the bus ride in, he kept thinking of how they had to do something, find out what the fake Tasha is doing. Obviously, going to the cops like Luna suggested is out of the question, but they can try to figure something out. They have to.

"What is happening?" Soledad asks, laughing. "Is this who you were hanging out with yesterday?"

Luna hesitates. "Not really."

Pedro leans on her desk. "Don't do this," he says. Rafa turns to face them.

"What is he talking about?" Soledad's loud enough to

get the attention of Isaac, who is about to saunter over. Pedro is more than ready. A fight may not be the right course, but at least it will help alleviate this tension he can't ignore. Everything is off, and the only two people who can talk about it are ignoring him.

"Everyone take your seat."

The teacher enters, and Pedro is forced to sit at his desk, angry at everything. Maybe it was just that, a bad hallucination? Maybe the house itself was filled with noxious fumes. Maybe years from now, doctors will detect a cancerous tumor lodged inside of him, and Pedro will know where it originated. From an evil girl who looked like someone he kissed a long time ago.

"Can I get the bathroom pass, please?" Pedro asks abruptly, standing up. He takes everything with him: his gold jacket, his messenger bag. Rafa looks at him as if he's about say something, but doesn't.

Unbelievable, Pedro thinks. *I need to get out of here before I scream.*

He enters the hallway with its rows of lockers on each side. He passes classrooms with their doors open, teachers scolding students to pay attention. Others enjoying their lessons.

"What am I even doing here?" Pedro says aloud. He heads to the main office, unsure what to do.

"What happened, Pedrito? You don't look like your usual sunshine." Amy, the school's receptionist, has known Pedro since middle school. Sometimes when he's late, Amy will let him go through without a tardy slip, that's how much she loves him.

"Can I just sit here? I'm not feeling well."

"Come on." She lowers the volume on a portable radio tuned to the news. "Is your uncle back?"

Although this is true, his uncle is back, it's not the whole story. Pedro nods.

"Just sit here, and help me stuff these envelopes. Remind me to write up your excuse for the teacher before the bell rings," she says. "Did you feel the earthquake? I'm waiting for the aftershocks. We have to be prepared."

Amy tends to another student, leaving Pedro alone with a stack of envelopes.

"There have been unusual sightings across the states."

Pedro turns the volume up on the radio. The reporter explains how tremors felt in California reached as far away as New Mexico. Others speak of unexplained lights blanketing the sky a couple of days ago.

"I saw them," Pedro says.

"Saw what, dear?"

"The lights. Didn't you?" he asks, but another student has entered the main office. Amy is once again preoccupied.

"Lights. Then Tasha," Pedro whispers. This is no coincidence. This is a sign.

Two white men in their thirties enter the office. One of them wears a suit; the other is more casual in a polo shirt with slacks. To Pedro, they both look like Jehovah's

Witnesses or computer salesmen trying to sell the school a new software upgrade.

"May I help you?" Amy asks. She too looks warily at them.

"We would like to speak to the principal," the man in the suit says.

For whatever reason, Pedro hides behind a computer. His instinct is ringing loud, and it's telling him not to get caught.

"Do you have an appointment?" Amy asks. She returns to her desk to grab her large, black scheduling book. When she does, Amy winks at Pedro.

"We spoke earlier. She's expecting us," the man in more casual clothes says.

"Your names?"

The serious one pulls out his badge. Pedro peers at the men while Amy leads them to the principal's office and shuts the door.

"I wonder what's that all about," Amy says, grimacing at Pedro. "I already need a break."

Pedro can't stop staring at the principal's closed door. He wishes he could listen in on the conversation, but it's not possible. He definitely shouldn't be here when those two come out of that office.

"I'm feeling better. I'm going to go back to class." He hands over the small stack of sealed envelopes to her.

"Okay, dear. There's always work for you here," she says. "Don't let your uncle bring you down. Remember you have options."

Yes, I do. A part of him thinks he should be documenting the events right now on his account like he always does. Evidence of the strangeness occurring. Another part of him thinks that to post anything will result in those two men finding him. He has no proof, but he feels this to be true. His gut is all that he has, and he's going with it.

We need to talk right now, he texts Luna. *Get Rafa and meet me behind the library, as soon as the bell rings, or I'm about to snitch on both your asses.*

Fine, Luna texts.

The bell goes off and Pedro waits, keeping a keen eye out for the two officers. Luna is the first to join him, with Rafa following close behind.

"What is it?" Rafa says, annoyed.

"What do you mean, what is it?" Pedro says, exasperated. "First, give me your number. I already got Luna's. We need to be in communication."

Rafa is reluctant but eventually tells Pedro his phone number.

"Second, cops are speaking to the principal right now, and I bet it has to do with a certain someone."

Rafa's face drops. He places his hands in his jean jacket. The second late bell will go off soon. "The cops could be here for any number of reasons," he says. "We did have a fight just a couple of days ago."

Pedro glares at him with one eyebrow raised high. "You're not that dense, are you?"

Rafa nervously cracks his knuckles. Because of this,

Pedro pulls out a stick of gum and hands one to Rafa and another to Luna.

"I can't stop thinking of her voice," Luna says. "It sounded so unreal. I keep hearing her."

"Not her. It," Pedro says. "Whatever it was, it wasn't Tasha. Call that thing for what it is—an unwelcome visitor. The Visitor that won't leave."

Luna chews her gum for a couple of bites and then tosses the candy out. "What if it was Tasha? Hear me out. What if it was her, and she has something to tell us?"

"Did you notice how the room was moving, like it was breathing?" Rafa asks.

"Breathing?"

"The house was completely empty two days ago. I know because I was there with her," Rafa says, continuing to crack his knuckles. "She, I mean, the Visitor made that happen."

Pedro pops another slice of gum in his mouth, thinks for a second, then pulls out another to chew on. "So, the message is it's going to kill us and make us one with the lawn? What are we even saying?"

"Shhhh."

All three of them look across to find their principal with the two officers. The "good" cop uses his hands a lot to express a point, while the serious one scans the area. Without having to say a word, Pedro and Rafa take cover behind a school sign detailing the night's football game. Luna does not.

"If they want to talk to us, we should go over there," she says. "Maybe they have answers."

"Do you want to get arrested?" Pedro says. "Is that it?"

"Luna, don't go speak to them. They will not help us in any way," Rafa says. "Don't do it."

Luna doesn't listen. She heads straight to the two cops, and all Pedro can do is watch.

"I'm not waiting for this to go down," he says and does an about-face. Rafa goes the opposite direction.

"It won't be the grass that kills her. It will be those two men." Pedro texts Rafa as he walks toward an exit.

CHAPTER 16

Pedro and Rafa may not trust cops, but what alternative do they have? These men may offer some clues. Let them think she's foolish. Luna doesn't care. At least she's taking some sort of action.

"Excuse me, Mrs. Walters," Luna says as she approaches the detectives.

"Miss Mendez, we were on our way to your class. These two gentlemen from the police force have a couple of questions for you," Principal Walters says. "Have you seen Mr. Estrada and Mr. Morales?"

"No, I haven't," she quickly says. Luna is smart enough not to turn to where she left them.

"Luna Mendez. It's nice to meet you," the casual cop says. "Is there a place we can chat privately for a minute?

Principal Walters pulls out a heavy set of keys and locates an empty classroom.

"We can use this room for a few minutes before the bell rings." She opens the door. "Miss Mendez, take a seat."

Luna sits in a chair while the adults stand. "How are you doing?" the casual cop asks.

"I'm fine." She smooths out her jeans and adjusts her top. She doesn't exactly have a plan. The impulsive act to speak to the two men came to her because of math. How else will she find out what's going on if she doesn't pay attention to the variables being presented to her? Luna needs answers, and they might have them.

Principal Water's walkie-talkie goes off. "I need to take this." She steps out of the open door of the classroom. She still faces them, so Luna doesn't feel completely alone.

The serious cop in the suit pulls up an image from his phone and shows it to Luna. The grainy image is of Tasha, and Luna's stomach sinks to the floor. They know!

"Have you seen this girl?"

"Last night. I saw her!" Luna is eager for answers, desperate for an explanation. "Who is she?"

"Where? What did she say to you?"

"Wait. Who is she?"

The serious cop already looks annoyed with Luna, so the casual cop takes over. Luna makes a mental note of this dynamic and how they're playing off each other.

"You and your friends are not in trouble. We are just trying to locate her. She's very sick," he says, cupping his hands together. "We need to get to her before she becomes too ill."

She's sick, of course, Luna thinks. Does she have the same illness that took Tasha? Almost everyone received the vaccine, but what if she didn't? Is this like some weird repetition, an echo of Tasha's ailments? A ghost stuck reliving the pain?

"She's real then," Luna says more to herself than to the cops, but she needs confirmation. "Right?"

The cop displays a concerned look to his partner then turns back to Luna. "Of course she is, but she's highly contagious. The longer she's out there, the worse her illness will become."

A weight lifts from her. To save this girl means to have a do-over, a chance to rectify her past mistakes. She might not be Tasha, but they've met for a reason.

"Who is she?" Luna asks again, and the serious cop answers.

"We understand you and your friends were trespassing. The owners provided us with footage from the security cameras."

"Oh" is the word that comes to Luna. A big, glaring *oh*. He is saying they are not in trouble, but that is a lie. They most definitely are, and Luna needs to pull back.

"What did she say to you?"

Luna wishes Mrs. Walters was back in the room with them. They both seem to be edging closer to her, and she feels claustrophobic.

"She didn't say anything," Luna says. They have the security tapes, so these two already know exactly what the girl said. They saw the way the room was overrun with plants, and they sure as hell saw when she was grabbed by the branches and lifted.

"The girl said she was hungry. She was looking for food and a place to crash," Luna lies. "I think she was on drugs. That's all."

"Something else happened. Before the earthquake," the serious cop says.

"Are you LAPD? What division?" Luna knows a thing or two about cops from her Uncle Johnny. He worked for years at Division 4 before he quit. Police officers have always been part of her family, and she's heard all about their tricks. Tasha and she have never had a fear when it came to cops until the uprisings against police brutality began in the city. That's when Tasha started questioning everything. The arguments she had with her parents became really heated. She told Luna all about it.

"Protecting her will only get you and your friends in trouble."

They are liars, and Luna needs to shut up. How unbelievably cliché this interaction is.

Principal Walters returns. "Sorry, gentlemen, but we will have to move this back to my office," she says, leading them out.

"And the other two?"

"We haven't located them yet, but they are bound to show up," she says.

As they walk together toward the main office, Luna notices a horrible energy emitting from these two men. A low, buzzing alarm alerting her to run.

"I need to get something from my locker," she says.

"This won't take long. We just have a few more questions, then you can go right back to class."

"Maybe the better solution is to bring her to the precinct. We can show her the tapes," the casual cop says as they arrive at their destination.

"We need to have a further discussion on transferring any student off this campus. While they are here, they are my responsibility," Mrs. Walters says. She places a reassuring hand on Luna's shoulder. "Luna, have a seat. We will get back to you."

Luna sits as the adults relocate to the principal's office.

"She's real," Luna says to herself. She's not a ghost or something they hallucinated. The men may be lying, but at least they confirmed that much. The fake Tasha is real, and they don't know where she is.

Amy, the receptionist, gives her a reassuring wink. Luna needs to get out of there. And fast.

CHAPTER 17

Rafa waits outside the Fairfax library for it to open. There are others standing with him, the library regulars who spend their days reading the newspaper and using the computers.

He looks down to his sneakers when the young librarian greets him with suspicion. Rafa has spoken to her a couple of times before when he needed to complete a school project. The librarian might call the dean on him, and she would have every right to turn him in for being truant, but Rafa doesn't have much of a choice. He needed to leave the school. This was the quickest solution that didn't involve hiding in Starbucks, a place truant officers are always patrolling. Who would go to the local library when they are cutting class? No one really, except for Rafa.

This library is not spacious enough to truly conceal him, but it will have to do while he waits for the right time to go home. He picks a seat in the far corner where he can still keep an eye on the door. What was Luna thinking, speaking to the cops? She must live in another space and time. Absolutely nothing good will come of it. What a mess he's made of things. Jeopardizing his family by getting involved.

After leaving the Gonzalezes this morning, Rafa walked his sister to school and urged her not to speak to any strangers. "Run if someone weird approaches you, especially a girl," he said. Mónica didn't understand, but she promised. Rafa has checked on his parents twice already. His father seemed concerned but not enough to question Rafa's actions. At least his mother and Mónica will be spending another night with the Gonzalez family. Rafa will return to their tent with his father tonight.

"They say it was four point five. It felt stronger to me." Two librarians speak softly as they shelve books. "It lasted for so long. I'm surprised more books didn't fall."

Rafa doesn't search for earthquakes on the library computer. Instead, he looks for any other occurrences. Nothing stands out except for a brief article from a couple of days ago on strange lights "across multiple states." He finds nothing about a girl.

Soon the heaviness of last night starts lulling him. His whole body is still so tense. The silence of the library is soothing. He rests his chin on his arm and closes his eyes.

"You can't sleep here."

Rafa startles awake. He didn't realize he had fallen asleep. In his dreams, he was right back in the house, trying to pull Luna from becoming part of a tree.

"I'm sorry," he says, wiping the drool from the side of his face.

"You should be in school," the librarian says with a cluck of her tongue. This is his one and only warning.

"I'm going back." Rafa quickly picks up his things. He doesn't want to cause any trouble. His whole life has been about blending into the background. Ever since last week, he's been doing everything but that. Being involved in a fight. Speaking to the strange girl. Taking Pedro and Luna to her. Earthquakes and now the cops. What is wrong with him? His only job was to stick to himself. To finish off this school year so he can hopefully find a job. The past week, he's found ways to jeopardize it all.

Rafa exits the library and keeps his head down. Only a couple of more hours before the end of the school day, then he will be in the clear. He can head back home and forget everything.

He takes a detour across Pan Pacific Park toward the outdoor stone steps that lead down to a large field where a group of men play a lively game of soccer. Rafa finds a bench nearby, trying to tag on with the adults. A couple of the soccer players give Rafa a nod hello. He feels safe among them. They won't call the police on him. They don't care if he's missing school.

The sun is high, and it's hot. Rafa peels his jacket off and rests it on his lap. Soon he finds himself relaxing as he watches the game. He's not sure who he's rooting for, but he likes that even in this park, older men who look like family are enjoying a weekday break. Not everything is about work. Even these men can take a tiny respite from the constant struggle.

"¿Juegas?" a man seated next to him asks.

"No tengo las piernas," Rafa jokes.

He's never been much into sports. Playing a sport always entails spending money he never has. He looks up to allow the sun to blanket his skin for a few seconds.

A shadowy silhouette approaches the field from the Third Street entrance of the park. The hairs on the back of Rafa's neck stand up. The man continues to tease him about not playing soccer, and Rafa pretends to listen, all the while his eyes stay glued on this person. The figure takes shape.

It's her. The fake Tasha walks down the small hill toward the field.

Rafa jumps up.

"¿Pasa algo?" the man asks. He sees the young girl. "Ah. ¿Tu novia?"

He kids some more, but Rafa's not laughing. He is horrified. She's found him.

The fake Tasha slowly walks across the field, disrupting the game. The players scream at her to move out of the way. She is laser focused on Rafa, and he doesn't want to find out the reason why. He quickly moves and heads north, away from her.

He thinks of going to Fairfax Avenue when he sees a patrol car driving down Beverly Boulevard. Rafa ducks behind large garbage bins in the park's lot and waits a few minutes until the cop car drives past. He crosses and enters a residential street.

I need to warn them. Rafa takes out his relic of a cell phone, finds Pedro's earlier text to him, and types two words only: *She's here.*

He doesn't wait for a response. He has to keep moving. Rafa turns and sees the girl calmly walking toward him. Where can he go? Without thinking, he heads back to school. At least there will be people there. Maybe he can lose her in the droves of students.

"Hey, Estrada! Where are you supposed to be?" the dean yells from the south gate entrance of the school. "Get in here right now."

In the corner of his eye, Rafa sees the girl just a couple of streets away.

"Let's go!" the dean says, opening the gate. "Principal Walters has been looking for you. Where's your partner, Mr. Morales?"

"I don't know. I'm going to class right now." Rafa wants him to close the gate after him. The dean doesn't notice the girl yet.

"No, not class. Main office right now." He uses his walkie-talkie to alert the office Rafa is on his way. "Do I need to escort you there?"

"No, sir," Rafa says. The girl is just across the street from the school.

The dean now turns to the fake Tasha, who continues forward. Rafa hears him yell at her to get to class as he heads in the direction of the main office. Rafa peeks into Principal Walter's window. The two white men from earlier are in there talking to her. He will not fall for whatever is waiting for him at the principal's office.

Where can I go? Rafa frantically thinks. He checks his phone, but there are no messages. He texts Pedro again and turns back to look for the girl.

"Watch where you're going!" Isaac shouts.

CHAPTER 18

Isaac noticed Rafa turning the corner, leaving himself wide open for a push. It's not his fault if Rafa is too distracted to pay attention.

"Have you seen Luna?" Rafa asks.

This guy really doesn't get it. Isaac heard all about how Rafa and Luna were hanging out yesterday. He called Luna a couple of times last night to no answer. When Isaac asked her this morning where she was, her expression was enough to shut him up. Isaac doesn't get why Luna is friendly one day and cold the next. It's fine if she doesn't want to go out, but he really doesn't understand what she's doing with this guy. Rafa's a nobody and now he's in his grill as if they're cool.

"Get out of my face," Isaac says. His two friends laugh beside him. If he has to check Rafa, he will. It would be no problem.

"It's important I speak to her." Rafa looks around frantically. Maybe Luna shot him down like she does most guys. The thought makes Isaac happy.

"Get out of here, bro, before I make you," Isaac says before heading to the football field where the coach is waiting to start practice. Although he didn't start the fight with Pedro at the observatory, he still got a good talking-to this morning from coach. "One more fight and you are off the team," he said, and Isaac believes him. Football is the only thing Isaac likes. He's good at it even if their team isn't all that great. He can't mess this up.

Rafa calls out from behind him, "You don't understand. I need to find her and Pedro."

Isaac turns and gets right in Rafa's face.

"Stay the fuck away from Luna," he says. "Your sorry ass can't compete, so don't bother."

But Rafa isn't even looking at him. Isaac is at a loss. How is he supposed to convey fear if Rafa doesn't seemed to be fazed by his threats?

"Fuck this." Isaac gives up and leads his friends to the crowded football field. Beside the team, cheerleaders practice a dance routine while other students congregate in the stands working on posters announcing an upcoming school dance. Isaac picks up the pace and waves at the coach, proving he's following orders and not wrecking his chances. Rafa walks alongside them as if he's part of the team.

Isaac scans the field for Luna, wondering where she is. Then he stops himself. He's thinking like a desperate dude, always hoping for some scraps Luna might leave him. Isaac can go out with anyone he wants. Luna isn't the only person in this school.

Rafa bumps into him again, almost making him trip.

"She's here," Rafa says, his voice a tremor of fear. What is wrong with him?

"Dude, are you high?" Isaac asks. Rafa is scared, and Isaac doesn't get why. "Luna's not here."

"Hey, Isaac. Doesn't that girl look like Tasha?" his friend says.

Whoa. The girl looks just like Tasha, *just* like her.

"That's wild," Isaac says and grins. *Imagine that? I guess Rafa did see a wannabe Tasha.* The girl walks to them, a smile on her face.

What a trip.

At the opposite end of the field, the dean enters with two white men who are definitely cops. Things begin to click for Isaac. Something is not right, not with the girl heading their way and definitely not with the cops. That's for damn sure.

"Rafa, son, get over here." The dean speaks into a megaphone.

"I got to leave," Rafa says. He's desperate. "But where do I go?"

"Bro, what is going on?" Isaac asks. He may hate Rafa for whatever reason, but Isaac's no snitch. Fuck those cops walking across their football field. They don't belong in this school, and they sure as hell don't have the right to talk to anyone, even Rafa.

"Bounce, or we're all going to catch this heat." Isaac nods at him to head south, away from the cops and the girl who looks strangely like Tasha.

"Hold it right there!" the detectives yell, pulling out their guns as soon as Rafa takes a step.

"Oh shit! A gun!" Isaac shouts. Students immediately scatter, screaming. The dean tackles the cop wearing a suit, protecting the students, but the other detective runs forward with his gun pointed.

"Don't move!" the cop yells. He is quickly upon them, the gun cocked. Isaac and Rafa do as they're told. This isn't the first time LAPD has pointed a gun at Isaac but it will never cease from being the most terrorizing thing to experience. There's nothing he can do but wait with Rafa as the angry white man barrels toward them.

"The earth," Rafa says, and that's when Isaac feels it. Beneath their feet, the ground begins to shake. An incredible wind blows from out of nowhere. Isaac and Rafa find themselves trying to stay upright.

"Oh shit," Isaac says.

The policeman turns his gun to the young girl who looks like Tasha. She is only a few steps away from them. The girl smiles at the cop.

"Don't move, or I'll shoot!" the detective yells, no longer interested in the two boys.

A giant tidal wave of dirt emerges from behind the officer. It grows larger and larger as it speeds over to them. Isaac is mesmerized by what he sees.

"Run, Isaac!" Rafa yells. "Run!"

CHAPTER 19

Pedro is practically off campus when he changes course. A little voice in his head reminded him of something Tasha told him the night they hung out at the Grove. It was after the movie but before they kissed. She said Luna was more than just her cousin. She was her sister, and if anything happened to her, Tasha would destroy everything and everyone who did her harm.

"Luna thinks she's strong, but she's not. She follows my lead," Tasha said. "I need to push her out of her bubble or else she will be stuck there."

Instead of walking through the exit, Pedro makes an about-face and retraces his steps. He catches up to Principal Walters, Luna, and the two men as they turn into another hallway.

Pedro keeps his distance, but he still follows the group as they enter the main office. He waits by the door, listening in.

"We'll be done shortly," the principal says.

The two men enter Mrs. Walter's office, leaving the door slightly ajar.

As Pedro creeps in, he presses a finger to his lips, alerting Amy not to make his presence known. And because she always has Pedro's back, Amy does just that. In fact, she gets up, walks over to the principal's office and asks her a question.

"Come on," Pedro whispers to Luna. He pulls at her hand, and Luna follows him out of there. They push through the main exit of the school and keep running.

"They wanted to take me in," Luna says, out of breath. "They kept saying I was in big trouble. But I didn't do anything."

Pedro smacks his lips.

"We told you not to talk to them, but you thought better," Pedro says. He heads toward Fairfax, where most of the sneaker heads are lining up for the latest brand about to drop any minute.

"I thought they would help," Luna cries out.

"When has anyone in an ugly, cheap suit ever been helpful?" Pedro asks. He leads her to a sneaker store he's been to hundreds of times. "Go inside."

He nods at the security guard, who allows them in. Pedro knows everyone on Fairfax. He also knows that the back of this store has a selfie gallery for people to pose. They can hide there.

Inside the gallery are multiple mirrors in various shapes. It is a small room made to look like a funhouse. Luckily, the room is empty.

"He kept asking where she was."

"Then they think the Visitor is dangerous," Pedro says.

"I don't know. They asked me when was the last time I saw her and what did she say." Luna wipes the sweat above her brow. "They weren't interested in the house or anything like that. They said she's sick."

Pedro stops and thinks this through. Conspiracy theories have never been his thing. Back then, everyone had their theories about the virus. Everyone. But he believed it was just that, a virus that attacked and they didn't find a cure until it was too late for many. What is the conspiracy behind this Tasha?

"They don't know what's going on," Pedro says. "We know more than those pigs."

Pedro can feel Luna's anxiety. They can't stay there for long.

"Did you mention us?" he asks.

Luna is unable to face him.

"Seriously? Jesus Christ," Pedro says. "Is this your first time at the rodeo or what?"

He is so angry. They'll be looking for him, and this will be yet another reason why he's a fuckup, another thing his uncle can use against him.

"They knew about you guys," Luna explains. "I couldn't just lie. There were security cameras."

"The real Tasha would never."

As soon as he says it, Pedro regrets his words. But it's too late. His life is in jeopardy because of Luna's saintly ways. Of course, she should have lied. Why couldn't Luna have kept his name out of her mouth?

"You don't know my cousin," Luna says. "You dated Tasha once and that's it."

"She sure as hell wouldn't have snitched," Pedro says. "She was right. You're too green, like a baby bird in a nest. Wake up, Luna."

"You spoke on the phone a couple of times with her, and now you think you're family? She thought you were a joke, like your clothes," she says. "At least I got information from the cops, which is more than what you did."

Pedro claps his hands enthusiastically. "Good work, Sherlock. Unbelievable. I should have left you back there. Wasn't it yesterday when I saved you from becoming one with the trees? How many times people got to be looking out for you before you return the favor? Tell me so I can adjust my expectations."

Luna snatches her bag and heads to the door.

Pedro might have pushed too far, but someone has to be honest with Luna, because her friends sure aren't.

A quick glance in the mirror, and Pedro's face appears distorted. Ugly. He doesn't want to be this way, but why does his mouth always shoot first? Lash out to cause as much hurt as possible? Just like his uncle.

Pedro runs after Luna. He doesn't have to go far to find her. She is frozen in front of the large storefront windows.

"Look," she says.

Pedro follows Luna's trembling finger. His blood freezes.

The Visitor walks in the middle of the street. A long

line of cars are stuck behind it with drivers honking their horns to get out of the way.

"That girl wants to get hit by a car," the store's security guard says. "It's always something with you kids."

The guard adjusts his belt and heads out.

"Don't go out there," Pedro pleads with him. "The girl, she's not right."

"Exactly." The guard leaves anyway. He tries to direct the strange girl toward the sidewalk. The fake Tasha stops dead center on the avenue.

They should run, get away from this thing, but Luna and Pedro can't peel themselves away from the window.

"This can't be happening," Pedro says. The hairs on his neck bristle as if called to attention.

The guard reaches for his radio all the while the Visitor ignores the blaring horns and the increasing commotion. Bystanders venture out from nearby stores, wondering what is wrong.

Soon, a string of cop cars speed up the avenue. Pedro thinks the guard must have called them for help, but that is not the case. These cops are arriving because of the violent incident at Fairfax High School that Pedro doesn't know about yet.

Patrol cars quickly block off Beverly Boulevard. Policemen spill out with their batons ready. It's been a while since Pedro has seen so many cops on Fairfax Avenue. It happened once before when Young Cash decided to give a free concert, causing a bit of a riot. Then there were the BLM marches. It's all too fresh still.

An LAPD officer approaches the Visitor.

"Tasha," Luna whispers as if she's oddly issuing a warning.

"We need to go," Pedro says.

They step out of the store, blending in with the crowd.

"Come with me," the cop says. She reaches for the fake Tasha, but when the officer touches its arm, the cop begins to cough uncontrollably. She hacks and struggles to breathe. The cop bends over for a few seconds then lifts her head. She opens her mouth wide, unnaturally wide. The cop's body spasms as if she is about to throw up, when a large branch shoots out of her mouth, tearing open her skin. The police officer collapses.

Her partner pulls out his gun from his holster, but his hands are no longer hands. They are now branches so heavy, he falls to his knees.

Luna screams, and the fake Tasha turns to face them, a chilling smile present. Pedro yanks at Luna, pulling her to run with the panicked crowd.

Another cop: His chest explodes in vibrant flowers. Blood, entrails, and petals spill out on the avenue. Shrieks and shooting mix together for a thrumming soundtrack.

The cops—unsure who the culprit is, because surely it can't be this young girl—turn to the people trying to get out of the way. They start using their batons. Every-one runs, shielding themselves from the shots and the detonating bouquets of anatomy. Another cop goes down, and his eyes are now thorns.

"Shit, shit, shit, shit," Pedro says.

There are multiple streams of chaos. Pedro and Luna can barely hold on to each other, their hands clasp so tightly.

"Where do we go?" Luna yells.

"Just move!" They turn on Rosewood Avenue and head west with so many others. Kids from Fairfax High School join them, scared or laughing, not knowing what is happening.

The Visitor is undaunted. It walks up Fairfax Avenue. More cops fall. A leg is rooted to the ground. Another officer's back is ripped apart. Another screams in agony as his hand is no longer a hand but a passionflower with purple and white petals.

Pedro and Luna keep running.

CHAPTER 20

Luna digs her nails into Pedro, afraid to let go. The rush of people bump into her, almost causing her to fall, but she rights herself and keeps going. Luna pushes the horror she just witnessed out of her mind and only focuses on her feet on the ground, on getting away.

Ambulances careen across the more popular streets. Innocent bystanders walking their dogs cling to their animals, unsure what to make of the commotion. They've never seen so many people crashing their quiet residential streets.

"Oh my god," Luna says.

"Don't think, just move," Pedro yells. And she does that, holding on to him.

Eventually, the large group dwindles as others take off to side streets, but the hysteria percolates like a kettle whistling. Luna and Pedro slow down their pace, enough to catch their breath and check for signs of the girl.

"Luna! Pedro!"

A familiar voice calls to them.

"It's Rafa!" Pedro says. They step aside, allowing the others to go through while they wait for Rafa to catch up. When he reaches them, Rafa's face is covered in dirt. His eyes bloodshot.

"You saw her," Luna says.

"At the football field," Rafa says. "It was so sudden. A bunch of wind. I couldn't see anything. Just a dust storm. And when it stopped, the players were gone. The coaches. Nothing left but large mountains of dirt."

"She made the cop's body explode," Luna says, then she covers her mouth in shock.

"Come on," Pedro says.

"Where?" Luna asks.

"The Beverly Center," he says without hesitation. "It's big enough. There are bathrooms. Food. Well, some food."

The food court on the last level of the Beverly Center used to be a place to hang out, but they tore it down to replace it with upscale restaurants. No cheap Chinese food or pizza or tables for students from the neighborhood schools to occupy for hours on end. The mall only caters to rich tourists, not kids who want to share a couple of slices of pizza between four people.

"The mall is by the hospital," Luna says, and her mind turns to her mother, although her mother doesn't work at Cedars-Sinai Hospital. "It's going to be busy."

"Exactly," Pedro says. "The cops are going to be too tied up with that."

"I need to get a hold of my family." Rafa's hands

shake as he tries to locate his phone. Luna does the same thing. Her eyes dart about frantically, afraid the fake Tasha will appear any minute.

Pedro places his hand on Rafa's shoulder. "We will do this at the mall. Free Wi-Fi. Will you both just listen to me? Come on."

They begin again, not running as before but walking quickly, ignoring the strange stares from confused people. They avoid the main avenues where police create roadblocks a mile away, asking for identification from students and forcing them to stay where they are. Groups of scared kids wonder when they will be allowed to leave. Others weave in and out of the side streets, trying not to get caught.

It takes Pedro, Luna, and Rafa a little under a half an hour to get to the Beverly Center. Guards man the escalator that leads into the mall.

"They are not going to let us in. There's another entrance," she says, and they walk one block over to San Vicente, where a television crew is setting up. A representative from the mall alerts the crew as to the best angle for their shot. The exchange is enough for the three to enter through the parking lot that faces the hospital. They keep their heads down and avoid eye contact.

Inside, people go about their shopping business. Tourists sit at various public sofas. Others enter the luxury brand-name stores or take selfies in front of large-scale "experiences."

It's been a couple of months since Luna visited the

mall. It's just way easier to go to the Grove, the outdoor complex near her school. Although the Beverly Center recently updated its look, the place always feels so old-fashioned. Not hip enough for any of her friends to spend time there. The Grove is for them, the Beverly Center is for their moms and family visiting Los Angeles for the first time.

Without saying a word, the three locate a bathroom and walk into the ones labeled for their respective genders. Luna takes the stall farthest away. She presses her body against the door and silently cries into a wad of tissue. Her voice trembles no matter how deep she tries to inhale.

Luna waits for an older woman to leave the bathroom before she steps out. In front of the sink, she places her hand under the running water and washes away the tears.

What did she see? The cops became something else. The carnage. Luna didn't black out this time. Her eyes were wide open, watching a horror film she couldn't look away from.

It takes a long while for her to notice the phone vibrating in her bag. Her mother is trying to reach her.

"Baby, where are you?" her mother asks.

"I'm fine, Mom. I'm fine."

"They said there was a riot at Fairfax High School. You weren't a part of that, were you?"

"No, Mom. Of course not. I went to the mall. I'm with my friends. We are safe." She tries to keep from tearing up. She doesn't want to add to her mom's worry.

Someone calls out to her mother. It's Ceci. The phone sounds muffled.

"Baby, I need to get back. Go home as soon as you can. I don't want you to stay outside. Text me."

"I promise. I will text you when I'm home."

"I love you. Be safe."

"I love you too," Luna says, but her mother already hung up before hearing her words.

Did you keep your promise?

Tasha's voice floods her mind again like a sharp pain lodging itself in her body. Her heart hurts upon hearing it. A reminder of how she failed her cousin. The guilt never left, she just found ways to ignore it. By hanging out with Soledad and Isaac, she was able to conceal the wrong she did to her cousin. That circle of friends didn't care about the protests. They just wanted to be free of lockdowns and masks. But now, this thing, whatever it is, is here to bring Luna's regret back into focus.

A person enters the bathroom. Luna tries to compose herself, to shake off this dread. She splashes cold water on her face again and leaves.

Outside, Pedro hands her a bottle of water. Rafa speaks on his phone a little ways from them, but he soon joins the other two.

"How are you?" As soon as Pedro asks, she snorts in disbelief. "Never mind."

"I didn't know what to say to Mom," Luna says. She lowers her voice when a group walks past them, lining up to buy overpriced lattes.

"I hate cops, but that was something else, that was a whole other level," Pedro says.

"Did you see what happened? Their bodies were torn apart by trees." Luna stumbles over her words. "Unreal."

She tries to concentrate on the virtual "art" shifting and morphing into a type of silver liquid ocean. It's hypnotic enough to watch, this digital moving art piece controlled by a computer somewhere unseen. Every time Pedro speaks, she's aware of yet another aspect, and trying to process it renders her breathless so she stares at the altering video.

"At least my family is safe," Rafa says. "Are you going to check on yours?"

"My family? Yeah right. Let me focus on the people who actually care," Pedro says, and with that he starts recording himself.

"Stay the hell away from Fairfax Avenue and the surrounding areas. There is this girl, this monstrous thing. Don't approach her, don't even look her way. She's in the middle of this death spiral, and she's trying to take us all with her," he says. "I'm sorry to sound like I'm ringing the alarm for no reason, but it's true. The demon is wearing this."

Pedro motions to Luna to display the picture of Tasha on her phone.

"Stay away from the girl with pink hair. If you see that evil bitch, run. I'll check in with you later."

"Those cops will see that and look for us," Luna says, angry at Pedro's carelessness.

"Not the two men from school," Rafa says. "It got to them already."

"Híjole," Pedro says. "Still, I need to warn people. We all do."

"Not at the expense of our safety," Luna retaliates.

Pedro glares at her.

"I don't understand you. I saved your ass back there, and now you would rather not let others know of the danger. You were so quick to blab to the cops, and now you prefer keeping quiet. You're so misguided."

Luna opens her mouth then closes it. What is there to say? Her arguing with Pedro seems like such a frivolous act. She is stuck with these two strangers. Rafa, who hardly shares a thing, and Pedro, who never shuts up.

"Stop acting like you're an expert on me or Tasha," she says.

"Tasha! Why are we even talking about Tasha?" Pedro yells. "She's not Tasha. You don't know what that evil Visitor is."

"Neither do you!" she yells. *The Visitor?* You sound ridiculous."

Rafa hushes them both, but they are not listening. Anger builds up at unresolved situations from the past and their current predicament. Of being neglected and of missing this ghost.

A new set of security guards start to gather. One of the men points to them.

CHAPTER 21

A woman sits on a high stool with her eyes closed, allowing the makeup artist to dab bright-green eyeshadow on her eyelid. The woman in the seat reminds Rafa of his abuela, a person he spent countless hours with before she passed away. His grandmother wasn't friendly, and she rarely spoke. When she did, her pointed words were usually a command, but she loved Rafa, and he loved following her around, content with being quiet. Rafa was twelve when she died, and soon after, his family moved to Los Angeles.

"That green looks good on you," Pedro says, and the makeup artist beams with pride. The old lady doesn't smile. She clucks her tongue, a sign for the artist to continue her work. Just like how his grandmother would have reacted, Rafa thinks. The stern expression on this old woman also reminds him of Mónica when she's trying to concentrate. It's strange how Rafa is being met with this vision of his abuela and Mónica, right in the middle of Macy's, while dodging mall cops.

He follows Luna, who weaves through the aisles of makeup and perfume. At the far end of the store, she ducks into a dressing room. After pretending to browse at a rack of overpriced jeans, Rafa heads to the unmanned room as well, with Pedro waiting a few minutes to join them. Luna selects a stall toward the back. Before they close the door, Pedro locates an "Out of Order" sign and hangs it in front of the stall.

"I guess this is our new home," Rafa says, and it's the first almost joke he's shared. Pedro smiles at him.

Pedro pushes aside a long, black gown left hanging in the stall to sit on an ottoman. "What a mess. Retail work is the worst," he says. "The amount of trash you have to put up with is not worth the pathetic discount."

"And working at In-N-Out is better?" Luna says.

"All the burgers you can eat," Rafa says. "I would be okay with that."

"Working in the service industry is probably the worst thing you can do," she says.

Pedro scrunches his face. "You ever worked an actual job before, or is this pure speculation?"

Because Rafa can sense the discussion heating up again, he holds his hand out for them to stop. "Don't. I want to focus on getting out of here alive with less reality-show bickering."

"Reality-show bickering," Luna says. "Funny, Rafa, funny."

"I'm fine with being quiet until the coast is clear," Pedro says.

Luna takes to her phone, as does Pedro, but Rafa catches them sneaking glances at him when he's doing the same to them. Rafa never would have imagined this was how he would spend the past couple of days, with these two vastly different people. They are both beautiful and annoying. Mónica would have liked them right away. Rafa hates not being with her.

He takes off his jean jacket, which is still covered in dust. He places it on his knees and rests his chin on the fabric. Exhaustion hits him hard. The dull, buzzing sound coming from the central air is relaxing. Sleeping in strange places has never been a problem for Rafa, and he gives himself permission to rest his eyes, if only for a moment.

In this unrestful dream, his abuela appears, standing beside the dangerous Tasha. Rafa screams for her to run, but he finds himself stuck in a glass case. His grandmother scrunches up her face in confusion. Red orchids circle around her swollen ankles, slowly creeping up her legs. Her palms face out and dark-red flowers wrap around her arms. Rafa pounds on the glass frantically, trying to find an escape.

"Let her go!" he yells, but his voice comes out quiet.

The fake Tasha flashes her eerie grin. It stares at Rafa while his abuela becomes distraught and makes gagging noises. Rafa strikes at the glass box, and a crack slowly forms. He strikes again and again until his hands bleed. He must save his grandmother. And Mónica, where is Mónica?

When his abuela opens her mouth to scream in agony, petals drip out and float up to a dark sky.

Rafa jolts awake, drenched in sweat, his breath ragged. Disoriented, he takes a few seconds to find his bearings. When he does, both Pedro and Luna are deep in sleep. He slowly stands. He needs to get out of there.

On his call earlier, Rafa urged his father to take shelter with the Gonzalez family. It wasn't an easy task. His father didn't want to be a burden.

"You have to. There is something dangerous. Algo raro," Rafa said. "You need to stay inside."

Rafa hated being so vague with his father, but the coded sentences were more than enough. His father heard him.

"¿Cuando vienes?" he asked.

"Esta noche. Te mando un texto," Rafa said. "Si no puedo llegar, me quedo con mi amigo Pedro."

"¿El mismo muchacho de la pelea?" his father asked, confused. There was no time to explain why Rafa was with the boy from the fight. His father agreed to go to the Gonzalezes' and Rafa felt less anxious.

The dream fills him with dread. He's never suffered from nightmares, not even as a little kid. He needs to get out of here. This doesn't feel any safer than being outside with that thing. At least on the streets he can move. This is a cage.

Rafa heads to the door, slowly closing it behind him.

If he leaves now, he might be able to get to his family in an hour, provided the streets aren't cut off by the cops. He takes a few minutes to figure out how to get out of

Macy's. The Beverly Center is just one big shopping maze. He's so disoriented. It takes him another few minutes to find the elevator.

"Rafa!" Luna calls to him, startling him. "Are you just leaving us?"

"We can't stay in there forever," he says. "It's not safe hiding in this mall. I don't even know where the exits are."

"I do, and we're not planning to stay here forever, just long enough to avoid whatever is out there," Luna says. "I can't believe you were just going to leave. At least I woke up Pedro to tell him I was stepping out. You didn't even bother sending a text."

She walks ahead of him and angrily presses the elevator button. "I'm getting food. You can do whatever you want."

Rafa doesn't say a word. He doesn't feel the need to explain himself. They both enter the elevator, and when it reaches street level, Luna exits first and enters a restaurant called Eggslut. There are still so many cop cars and ambulances racing across Beverly and San Vicente. The commotion is now punctuated with helicopters hovering above them. Cops direct bystanders to avoid stagnating on the street.

"I need to cross," Rafa says to a cop, but the man just points him right back to the mall. It's not possible. He's stuck, just as he feared.

"Move," the cop says, and Rafa does that. He enters the restaurant and finds an empty chair facing the various screens tuned to the news featuring reporters trying to make sense of it all. Confusion is not just relegated to Los Angeles but New York, Chicago, Texas. Each state finds itself facing this unknown catastrophe. A mixture of the natural and unnatural. Violent attacks by unknown assailants. Words like "terrorism" and "biological warfare" are being tossed around by experts.

"Unreal," Luna says when she sits next to him. She places a drink in front of him and Rafa is grateful that she's not making him feel foolish for trying to leave. They watch the terror being documented in small towns and big cities.

"It's happening everywhere," Rafa says. "It's not just us."

The experts being interviewed on the screen offer no clues, just a lot of big words that mean nothing and only add to the confusion.

"What if we're the only ones who were able to talk to her?" Luna asks.

"*It.* Like Pedro says, call it the Visitor, because that's what it is."

She turns to him. "The cops called it a 'her.' What if it's a person?"

"If it's a person, then it's a bad copy," he says. "An evil glitch."

"Or a reminder," she says. "Don't you get the feeling it's searching for us?"

"What does it want with—"

Luna and Rafa both jump from the pounding on the restaurant's window.

CHAPTER 22

Soledad spots Luna through the window and bangs on it to get her attention before rushing into the restaurant.

"Oh my god, I'm so glad I found someone I know," Soledad says. "Where have you been?"

She hugs Luna tight and then realizes who she's with.

"Oh," Soledad says. "Oh."

She knew it. Soledad had a feeling Luna was into the new boy. Why else would she be so upset about the fight? Sure, Luna said it was the missing photo or something like that, but a whole bunch of people saw her get on the bus with Rafa yesterday. And now here she is with him. This is so funny!

"Have you seen Isaac and the others?" Luna asks.

"Isaac? No, but I'm sure he's probably looking for you," Soledad says with a huge mischievous grin. "Quick, let's take a selfie and send it to him."

Luna pushes the phone away from her face. "I'm not in a mood for selfies right now. Not after what I saw."

"What? It was just a bunch of people screaming,"

Soledad says. "I didn't see a thing. The cops tried to stop me from walking home, but I got Dad to take care of that. People are out of control today."

Soledad was heading to the football field for cheerleading practice when a rush of students almost trampled her. She was so annoyed at having to walk back to her locker to get her stuff before the school went on complete lockdown. Either way, her plans were kind of ruined. Unable to get to her car, Soledad has been slowly walking home.

"Didn't you see what happened?" Luna says. "The girl, did you see the girl?"

Soledad doesn't know what she's talking about. Luna is always going off about one thing or another. It's hard to keep up. "What girl?"

"You didn't see her. You didn't see Tasha?"

Soledad starts to laugh. "What are you talking about?"

"She looks like Tasha," Rafa adds. "But she's not. We don't know what she is."

They are not joking, Soledad thinks. *They are serious.*

"Listen to us. This girl, thing, she looked exactly like Tasha," Luna says. "The cops came to the school, looking for her. And she turned them into branches."

"You both are so weird," Soledad says. She gets that Luna misses her cousin, but this is crossing a line. She hasn't been right ever since her cousin died, and now she's even seeing her. Luna needs to get a grip.

"She's telling the truth," Rafa adds. "Ask Isaac. He

saw her. We both did. And then this thing, this girl who looks like Tasha, made the ground shake. She created a dust storm."

Soledad's eyes go wide in disbelief. She didn't see any dust storm, and she definitely didn't see Tasha. Why is Luna listening to Rafa? Maybe he's the cause of all of this. She pulls Luna away from him.

"Luna, I don't think this is healthy," Soledad says. "Like, not at all. My house is five minutes away. You're welcome to come with me. I bet I can get the others to come over too. We can have a party!"

"You're not listening to me!" Luna grabs Soledad's arms. "You've got to stay off the streets. Don't go back outside. She's out there!"

The restaurant customers stare at them. This is not cool. Luna sounds hysterical.

"Let go of my arm. Tasha? Have you finally lost it?" Soledad says, losing her patience. Luna is so wrapped up in this new guy, she's not even making sense. "Jesus, Luna, get yourself together. There's no way you saw Tasha. It's not possible."

Soledad comes from a family of tough love. Rafa is probably humoring Luna because he wants to get some. Why else would he be spending all this time with her?

"Okay, you don't believe me. Fine. Just don't go back outside. Stay with us," Luna begs. "We're holing up in the Beverly Center until this blows over. Please, Soledad."

"I'm not going to the Beverly Center," she says. "Let go of my arm, Luna. You're embarrassing me."

"It's not safe out there! Please listen to me. This Tasha is killing people."

"Let go! I get you miss your cousin, but this is truly disgusting," Soledad says. "Your cousin has been dead for what, two years now? I can't believe you are using her memory like that, for sympathy or something just as pathetic."

Luna lets go of Soledad's arm. She's on the verge of tears, and Soledad feels justified for saying what she said because if it hurts, then it must be true.

"That's a horrible thing to say," Luna says, her voice cracking. "So what if Tasha's been dead for two years? Grief doesn't end no matter how many times you try to convince me to get over it. There's something out there that looks just like her. It's a warning. I'm begging you."

Rafa grabs a couple of bags of food. "We have to go," he says. "C'mon, Luna."

"You're seriously taking the side of some boy you barely know," Soledad says. "I wish it were Tasha out there, because she would never do that to me."

"I'm trying to do the right thing here," Luna says. "I'm trying to save you."

"I don't need saving! You're the one who keeps bringing up Tasha every five minutes. Now you're seeing her. If anybody needs serious help, it's you."

"You always made me feel bad for missing my cousin," Luna says, shaking her head. "We're going to leave."

Soledad can't believe what she's saying, the accusations. "Go then! Go. I'm good. Bye!"

Luna and Rafa leave the restaurant, and Soledad is completely at a loss.

"What just happened?" she says to the cashier who takes her order.

Soledad sits by the window and pretends not to be upset, but it's hard. How can Luna say those things, especially after all she's done for her? She tries reaching Isaac, but he doesn't answer. She texts other friends, asking them to come to her house.

The young man at the cash register loudly gasps, dropping Soledad's order to the floor. Soledad gets up, annoyed with her meal being screwed up. She pays no attention to the violence being enacted on the streets behind her.

CHAPTER 23

The scream wakes Pedro up from his brief nap. He fell right back asleep after Luna jostled him to tell him something he can't remember. Now he's alone in a Macy's dressing room. No Rafa or Luna, and someone nearby is screeching.

"Those fucks," he curses while grabbing his backpack and stumbling out the room. The blaring shriek continues. There are sounds of people running. He joins a few of the workers standing at the department store's entrance.

"Oh my god."

Pedro edges to the front of the small crowd to get a better view. He ignores the hollering white woman gripping a Gucci shopping bag to her body. Instead, Pedro holds his phone in front of him and presses record.

A mountain lion slowly lumbers past Victoria's Secret. The lion is unlike the ones usually found on the Santa Monica Mountains with code names like P-35 or P-21. At close to three hundred pounds and near five feet, the massiveness of the cougar is the first terrifying aspect. The second is harder to mentally grasp.

"Those aren't horns," Pedro says as he records. "Those are branches, like someone stabbed the lion on the side of its head."

He zooms in on the unnatural structure above the cougar's ears to show the texture and the disturbing amount of dried blood covering the tips. Tiny leaves hang off the outgrowth.

"I'm not playing with a filter. This is real. A scary hybrid animal has entered the mall like it's the new owner." Pedro calmly documents the scene, while all around him, people run for shelter.

A mall cop pulls out his gun, ready to shoot at the animal.

"You serious about that?" Pedro says, but the man ignores him.

The mountain lion leaps up on an elevated structure that marks a sitting area for shoppers. The slick, rectangular box is mirrored, revealing the mess of dainty, white flowers puncturing the cougar's skin. As the flowers brush against the surface, it leaves a thin layer of poison behind. Later, when a person lays a hand on it, if it is not thoroughly cleaned—which it won't be—the person's hand will instantly burn. Fever blisters will bubble up from their skin. The pain will be excruciating.

The cougar focuses on the man with the gun. It leans back on its hind legs, and the branches loom above them both. It's ready to leap onto the mall cop, and although

Pedro pleads with him to put his gun away, the man refuses to be intimidated by this unknown animal making its debut on level eight of the Beverly Center.

A shot goes off, and the cougar pounces. Pedro continues to record, but he's not even looking. He is unable to move. Unable to feel his legs. Two more mountain lions jump on the man. Pedro instantly feels the need to urinate, his bladder full.

"Pedro! Move!"

Rafa and Luna yell from across the way. Their voices snap him into action. He runs from the carnage, back to the dressing room, but another trio of mountain lions appears in front of Macy's.

Pedro veers left to the Dolce & Gabbana store and enters right before the retail clerk locks the doors shut.

"My friends," Pedro says as Rafa and Luna pound on the door. The clerk refuses to let them in.

"Open the fucking door right now, or I'm going to break the window." Pedro grabs a vase, dumps the flowers and water to the floor. The white man dressed in a slim dark suit sizes Pedro up, but Pedro knows he can take him. He will if he has to. The remaining customers yell at them to keep the doors closed.

"Open it!" Pedro yells. "Open it right the hell now, or I'll do it and we will all be fucked."

The clerk reluctantly opens the door a few inches, just enough for Luna and Rafa to squeeze through. The man quickly locks it behind them in time to see the cougar with the branches stomp menacingly. Someone screams from within the mall. The cougar heads toward the noise.

"Thanks for letting us in," Luna says, dripping with sarcasm.

"You can easily leave if you feel a certain way," the clerk says.

"You are not being paid enough to lord this over us," Luna says. "Jerk."

"Excuse me! Excuse me! We need to get out," a man standing alongside a woman dressed in a tight outfit and teetering heels demands.

The clerk immediately acknowledges the couple, walking them toward the back of the store. A few others follow them.

"Of course. I must not have the right skin color for them to treat me like a human," Pedro says loud enough. "And where the hell were you two? Woke up, and you were gone. You could have at least left me a damn note."

"I told you where I was going," Luna says. "I asked you if you wanted something to eat, and you said yes and then went back to sleep."

"And where is it?" Pedro asks. "The food?"

"I dropped the bags when I was running," Luna says. Pedro rolls his eyes.

Alarms go off throughout the mall. A voice on the intercom system alerts the customers to stay in place. Warnings of wild animals on the loose. The lights go out, and with the darkness comes more yelling and uncertainty.

"This won't end, will it?" Luna asks.

"It's just beginning," Rafa says.

The store is separated into a handful of actual customers, those who have spent hours in various high-end retail shops around the world, and on the other end, the three high school students. Pedro, Luna, and Rafa stare out into the chaos, each of them calculating the risks in leaving and finding only dead ends.

"At least we are in the dark, literally," Pedro says. He grabs a jacket from the rack, tears the tag off, and puts it on.

Rafa and Luna stare at him in disbelief. "What is he going to do?" Pedro says about the clerk, who is too busy placating the people with money. "Tell me to pay for it? He can take up a collection from them. Besides, I left my favorite gold jacket in the dressing room. Consider this emotional payback."

A mountain lion stalks the front of the Dolce & Gabbana. Blood covers the animal's jaw.

"Its eyes," Rafa says. "Look at them."

The cougar's eyes glow an unnatural blue. Luna's whole body begins to tremble. Pedro grabs a sweater from another rack and places it over her shoulders. He gently urges her to sit down with him. Rafa settles on her opposite side. Together, they watch the beast in horror.

"How can anything so vicious be so beautiful?" Pedro asks. "He must be a Leo."

Luna doesn't laugh. She leans into Pedro, placing her head on his shoulder.

"You can't wear those clothes." The clerk emerges after finishing catering to the other customers.

"Get the hell away from us, and never address us again," Rafa says with such an adult voice, it is shocking.

The clerk walks away in a huff.

Pedro was mad at Rafa and Luna for leaving him, but now? He can't believe what he just witnessed. This is a Rafa he didn't know existed, another side of him, and Pedro can't help but find this side to be hella fine.

"Wow, Rafa. You are giving me Mandalorian vibes right now," Pedro says. "I'm here for it. Just give me a warning next time so I can document your actions on video."

It's dark, but Pedro catches Rafa's smile. A silent exchange. There is something there, between them. He can feel it even in all this violence, and knowing this brings Pedro a sense of security. Rafa is near him and that matters.

The lion lumbers closer to the front door. It circles around and drops down as if it's now guarding the store.

"Welcome to the Beverly Center," a recorded voice announces on the store's speakers.

"I definitely feel welcomed," Rafa says.

Luna reaches her hand out, and Rafa takes it in his. The three hold each other while staring at the lion's steady breathing. Up and down. The white petals on its coat traveling like a metronome.

CHAPTER 24

Luna's hands become sweaty, and she feels embarrassed by it. She wipes them on her jeans and hesitates before placing them back atop Rafa's. She always used to hold Tasha's hands when they walked together, and Tasha would joke at how clammy they would get.

"I'm so hungry," Pedro says.

She digs in her bag and offers him a granola bar, which he takes. She gives one to Rafa too. "It's not the same thing as an Eggslut sandwich, but at least there's fiber. I actually hate these things, but Mom always packs them. It's her way of feeding me."

"They're okay," Rafa says, and Pedro agrees but says the bar leaves him thirsty. He locates bottles of water behind the store's register. He grabs three and hands them out.

"I used to love coming to the Beverly Center," Pedro says. "You can mark the amount of times I've fallen in love here. Now I will only see this place as the first time I came in contact with a Jellicle cat from hell."

"I'm not getting any connection." Rafa taps on his phone. "My phone is going to die soon."

Luna pulls out a charger, but they don't have the same compatibility.

"It's old," Rafa says. "I got if off the shelf of a museum."

"Like a lost artifact." Luna chuckles.

She notices how Pedro's nervousness reveals itself by him picking at imaginary acne on his face. Luna wants to tell him to stop, but she doesn't want to fully commit to this mothering role. It's easier to focus on them than it is on the beast right outside.

"I'm not sure about staying here," Rafa says.

Pedro points to the slumbering creature. "You want to try to outrun that? It's not possible. I'm not."

"They are bound to send someone to rescue us," Luna says.

"Oh, yeah, the cops. That always works out for us."

Luna is tired of being the only one who thinks of defending cops. She doesn't love the LAPD, but her family members all come from civil servant jobs. Nurses, EMT, police. Hard-working families who believe in their work.

"Not all cops are power-hungry militant fascists. I have family who work in the force," she says. "I think of what happened on Fairfax, and I feel like throwing up. No one deserved that."

"I can't believe you. Do you know how many times LAPD have helped me? Never. I just remember being stopped by them all the time, asked for ID, or getting pepper sprayed during the marches. That was fun," Pedro says. "God, Luna, sometimes it's hard to like you."

"Fuck you, Pedro," she says and gets up. "I need to pee."

"Come on," he says. "I need to pee too."

Luna lets Pedro lead the way in the dark, using his cell phone for light. When they reach the bathroom, the obnoxious store clerk is using it.

"Hello! Can you move it along?" Pedro bangs on the door. The man doesn't respond. Instead, Pedro and Luna hear the sound of someone sniffing.

"Is he crying?" Luna whispers.

"Definitely not crying. It's called self-medicating," Pedro says, lightly pushing his hip to Luna's and mimicking doing a line of coke. "You think he'll share?"

Luna covers her mouth to stifle a laugh. "Today is endless," she says.

The clerk opens the door and stomps off.

"I don't trust that guy. He's just waiting to feed us to the lions," Luna says, letting herself in. "Oh, there's only one stall."

"You go first, and I'll be the bathroom monitor in case that dick wants to take another line." Pedro faces the door to give Luna privacy. She goes quickly and flushes. While she washes her hands, it's Pedro's turn. She doesn't dwell too long on the shadows lurking in the corners.

Luna examines Pedro's reflection in the mirror while she waits for him to finish using the sink. Even in this barely lit room, Pedro is really striking. She can understand why Tasha was so into him.

"She really liked you, you know," Luna says. "Tasha was hoping it would work out."

"Is this the part where we confess our dreams and desires? I can't do it, not in the Dolce & Gabbana bathroom," Pedro says. "Besides, these lions have branches for horns and flowers sticking out from their sides. I'm not mentally prepared for this part of the dystopia."

"What else is there to do?" Luna says.

After Pedro stopped answering Tasha's texts, Luna placed Pedro in the category of someone who no longer existed. A person who hurt her cousin. Tasha never admitted this pain, but Luna felt it.

"You are always talking about falling in love with people. How could you not have fallen in love with Tasha?"

Pedro uses a napkin to slowly wipe his face and hands. Luna waits patiently for him.

"I don't know, Luna. I don't have the answer to any of it," Pedro says. "I fall in love because I'm desperate to connect with someone, just like you. It's all we are doing, isn't it? Tasha and I connected on a level, but she wanted something else. She was searching, like me, but I didn't have it, and I don't think she understood that, and maybe I couldn't explain it to her."

Pedro's words seem to echo off the bathroom walls.

"My love wasn't enough to protect Tasha," Luna says. "I think it's better to close yourself off to feeling anything."

"Damn. I know you're a sad girl, but this is too much," Pedro says. "Nothing is worth closing off. The love I have won't be crushed by my uncle or any inhuman thing out there. I have more than enough love to share. An abundance of love that will survive even this disaster. You do too."

Luna doesn't believe him. He grabs her chin, lifts it up to really look at her.

"Enough love for everyone," he adds. "You have to let people in, the right people. I see the way you hide yourself in that circle of crap. You don't shine there because they won't let you."

Luna slowly pulls away from him. She knows Pedro's never liked her friends, and maybe that is really why he didn't like Tasha. The choices people make are so predictable. This affection will end, and she will be alone.

"When this is over, we'll go back to ignoring each other like before, and you'll forget. We all will."

"Now that's your problem right there," Pedro says. "I'm not capable of hiding trauma neatly away like you do. I intend to shout this to the world until they get tired of hearing from me. Instead of pretending everything is alright, show your ugliness and pain, because at the end, who cares? At the end we're just food for the lions."

It's easy for Pedro to place his feelings front and center for all to bear witness. He's always been that way, but not Luna. She was fully aware of the deadline placed on her grief. She spent the past two years concealing her anger and sadness as much as possible. When Tasha was alive, she felt free. They could do anything. The future was right there for them to shape and mold. Then a virus no one understood took Tasha and Luna's courage away. There is so much anger within her over the unfairness of it all. How one person dies while others go on to feel joy and love, even rage.

The strange thing is that, deep down, Luna is secretly in awe of this fake Tasha. It is as if Luna's anger over Tasha's death is finally being manifested in real time by this alien ghost. A destruction Luna is both amazed and repelled by. These feelings are confusing her so much, and to reveal them now would show a hideous side Luna is not prepared to uncover.

"Forget it." She walks out of the bathroom and heads to the store's windows.

Did you keep your promise?

Luna closes her eyes, trying hard to drum out the voice of her cousin. The guilt adds to her confusion. She must right this wrong.

"Don't get mad at me for speaking the truth," Pedro says, going after her. "If this is when we confess, then let's confess."

"I don't want to talk anymore," Luna says.

"That's another reason why you are the way you are," Pedro adds. "You can't keep things bottled up. You're bound to explode."

Then, a familiar scent permeates the air. The cougar

sits up and stretches its massive body, looking bored. It turns and trots into the darkness.

Pedro continues talking. Luna stares intensely into the gloom of the mall, waiting for something to appear. A hint of excitement emerges in her, it's disturbing how much she is beginning to long for this feeling.

"I just think we should talk this out, because who knows how long we will be here? We're friends," Pedro says. "Are you listening to me? Jesus, what are you looking at?"

"Tasha."

The Visitor rounds the corner.

CHAPTER 25

The mountain lions brush against the Visitor's legs. The Visitor lightly caresses the tops of their heads.

"The light. Put your phones away," Rafa says. He runs to the back of the store with Pedro to notify the others.

"We are not opening the door for her," the clerk hisses. "I don't care who she is."

"Shut up," Pedro says. "Just turn off your phones."

Those in the back don't see the threat the way they do. With each step the Visitor takes, the shopping center becomes covered with plants just like the house it occupied. The escalators and the ceiling are slowly enveloped in a verdant landscape. Beverly Center is transforming into a breathing jungle, tangled and massive.

Rafa turns away from them and quickly rummages through the store's cabinets and drawers looking for anything he can use to protect himself. He finds only useless items like a stapler.

A scuffle ensues. There is the sound of a door

opening. The remaining customers, along with the store clerk, leave through the back door. Rafa chases after them, ready to bolt as well, but before he follows them through the exit, Pedro slams it shut.

"What do you think you're doing?" Rafa says. "We need to get out of here!"

"Wait! Listen!"

Rafa tunes into the noise. The vicious tearing sounds made by the beasts. The unnatural growls.

"We have to find a way out," he says, punching the door with his fist. His anger is overtaking his desperation. There must be a way out of this chaos.

"We do, but not through here," Pedro says and makes sure the door is locked. The two head back to the front of the store, trying their best not to bump into things in the dark.

Although the lights are out, a fantastical glow emanates from the Visitor, illuminating its steps and everything around it. The fake Tasha has its very own spotlight, and Luna appears to be amazed.

"Protect yourself," Rafa says to Luna, but she doesn't move. He shakes his head at Pedro, who also witnesses her enthralled state.

"Luna, we need to hide." Pedro grabs her by the shoulder to try to snap her out of it, but she won't budge.

"What if she wants to talk to us?" Luna asks. "What if she has a message for us?"

"Never mind the message. The Visitor can keep it."

Pedro leaves her and looks for a weapon. He grabs a broom handle.

There are more screams. Rafa pushes away the image of those people and their probable fate. The message the Visitor is sending is obvious: Death.

Like a snake, a vine slithers across the surface of the storefront. A crack emerges from the corner of the window. Then another. This crack spreads out until it becomes an intricate web. Rafa looks on in disbelief as Luna reaches out to touch the breaking surface.

"Get away from the window!" Rafa yells, but Luna ignores him. Instead, she presses her finger against the shattering glass.

Seconds later, the window explodes, propelling them all to the floor.

Broken glass is everywhere. Rafa searches for Pedro first, ignoring the drizzle of blood and tiny shards sprinkled across his face and hands. He finds Pedro cowering on the ground, examining his own injuries. They both then turn to Luna, whom they find face down. They drag her behind the store's register.

The glowing Visitor sits a couple of feet from the entrance of the store.

"Are you okay?" Rafa asks. Pedro replies with a yes, but Luna is silent. He asks again until she nods.

"What do we do now?" Pedro says. "I don't want to die in this fucking mall."

"I don't know," Rafa whispers. "I don't hear any more screams, which means—"

"RIP. Fuck, fuck, fuck," Pedro says, pulling at his cheek. "Remember when everyone wanted to be a plant mama? Now look at us, about to be killed by one."

Rafa huddles closer to Pedro, placing a hand on his wrist and gently pulling his hand away from his face. They can't afford to lose it. Not now. They need to survive this.

"Why are you doing this to us?" Luna shouts, startling them both. "Who are you?"

"Her name was Tasha," the Visitor says. Its voice has transformed again. This time it takes on the speech of the mall's recorded announcement. A ridiculous, peppy voice that's detached and fake in its welcoming tone. "I remember the pain. The noise from the machines. And your voice."

"Tasha," Luna says, turning to them for validation. "It's Tasha."

"No, it's not! She sounds nothing like Tasha," Pedro says. "Stop looking for something that's not there. It's not Tasha."

The two start bickering again.

"Why can't this be Tasha too?" Luna asks in between tears.

As they argue, Rafa cements his decision to leave. He has to stay alive, no matter what. So Rafa begins plotting his escape. He only hopes that Pedro follows, because Luna is lost in the memory of her dead cousin, and this will surely take them all out.

"It is only a matter of time before the others arrive," the Visitor says. "Then the conversion will begin."

"Others?" Rafa repeats, and he imagines an army of Tashas taking over.

"If there are others, where are they coming from?" Luna asks. "Are they dead too?"

There is a long pause with the only sound coming from their ragged breathing.

"From beyond your earth's atmosphere," the Visitor says with the saccharine voice of a person selling beauty products.

"I fucking knew it. A freaking alien from another planet," Pedro mutters to himself. "Nightmare. This is a nightmare. A worldwide conversion, and we're the guinea pigs."

"But it hasn't converted us yet," Luna says. "We haven't been turned into plants."

"You said it yourself right now," Rafa says. "Not yet."

He is calm because when you make the decision to live, those around you truly don't matter. His only thought is how he will run into the dark at the right moment. He hopes Pedro is thinking the same thing.

"You keep talking to her as long as you want, Luna," Rafa says. "I'm getting out of here."

"Me too," Pedro says.

"But we're the variables in this equation," Luna says. "Why is it just sitting there, talking to us? Why did it follow us here to the mall? There's a reason why. Don't you see?"

Rafa shudders. Variables. Luna believes in some sort of logical explanation, a clean-cut formula she can use to control this turmoil. The thing out there has all the power, and they are just three people stuck in a Dolce & Gabbana store.

But this is where Rafa carves another path, one where he lives in spite of that thing out there, whether it's a conjured ghost out for revenge or something they can't imagine.

He hunts in the cabinet beneath the register and finds hand sanitizers and cleaning wipes. Pedro joins him in the search, but it is useless. Then Rafa's eyes turn to the fire extinguisher hanging on the wall.

CHAPTER 26

Everyone has lost their damn minds, Pedro thinks. Even he has, because how is it possible he's not just pulling his hair out of his skull?

Luna is getting caught in this dangerous web as if she's being seduced. The Visitor isn't human. Who knows what its species is?

Pedro yanks Luna back down as she makes to walk toward the Visitor.

"What the hell do you think you are doing?"

"I'm talking to her," she says.

"What for? It's not like you can talk your way out of this."

"You don't know that."

"*YOU* don't know! This isn't *Lilo and Stitch*!"

The Visitor doesn't move. She flashes the same dead expression. An evil blankness.

"Why do you look the way you do?" Luna asks in spite of Pedro's hard glare.

The Visitor takes out the picture of Tasha and places

it in front of the cougar to sniff. Luna pulls away from Pedro. It is as if she's being drawn toward this thing like a magnet.

"Luna!" Pedro yells, to no avail. This girl wants to die. Why does she insist there's a connection when there isn't? It's only a violent illusion that wants to trick her.

Pedro turns to Rafa in despair.

"I'm getting out," Rafa says, and Pedro gets that this statement excludes Luna. Rafa is telling him because he is either following whatever plan Rafa is formulating or he's staying behind with Luna.

"We can't just leave her," Pedro says.

"You try to stop her." Rafa stays crouched down to the ground. He starts to crawl his way to the fire extinguisher.

Pedro pulls at Rafa's jacket to try to stop him. He peeks over to Luna, who is still speaking to the Visitor. The giant lion's head is tucked down, the same way a cat would fall asleep on its owner's lap.

"Is there a part of Tasha in you?" Luna asks. "There is, isn't there?"

Pedro holds his head. "Luna's asking journal questions to an alien ghost, and Rafa wants to try his luck out there with the lions. I'm surrounded by two reckless people when everyone probably would have assumed I would be the wild one."

He curses and joins Rafa, who holds the fire extinguisher, getting ready to use it.

"You said it yourself, you can't outrun them giant cats," Pedro says.

"Maybe I can spray them out of the way," Rafa says.

"Don't be an idiot, idiot." Pedro points back to the two figures, an alien who glows unnaturally and a girl who appears to be drowning. "You'll be killed by a tree branch. Plus, we can't leave Luna. We just can't. She's not thinking straight."

"Luna is about to get herself and us killed," Rafa says. "We have to think about us. Just come with me."

Pedro gives in to the nervous laughter bubbling inside. This beautiful boy in front of him is trying to save him, but Luna needs saving too. This journey thrusted the three of them together. They can't abandon her with this evil thing.

"I'm going to bring her back," Pedro says. "I'm begging you to wait before you make your move. Please."

It takes a few seconds, but Rafa eventually agrees. "Five minutes only. Then I'm taking my chances and running out the front."

Pedro gives Rafa a quick hug before standing up. His knees buckle a few times as he walks toward Luna and the Visitor. Pedro's afraid he'll be attacked by a lion—not just the one slumbering beside the fake Tasha but any surely lurking in the dark. He takes small steps, quiet as he possibly can.

"Luna," he says, almost in a whisper. She looks at him but doesn't seem to recognize him. It is as if she's drugged. "Let's go back inside, Luna. We can talk from in there."

The lion makes a low, rumbling sound like a train, and Pedro stops. He's only a couple of steps away from Luna, within arm's reach, but the lion's growl is a warning he heeds.

The Visitor's sinister smile is back, but it is not as intense as before, or maybe Pedro is simply getting used to it. This is a mask, he tells himself. A costume like any other costume. A borrowed skin.

He takes a moment to survey the destruction around him. Its army of beasts lounges about. There are various bodies splayed on the floor. It's hard to see because of the darkness, but he can tell by the silhouettes. He also discovers the creeping flora, the same that covered the house when they first met this pretend Tasha. Soon, Dolce & Gabbana will be hidden within the green.

The Visitor caresses the slumbering lion. Petals fall from the animal's sides. The flowers have strips of neon pink, and the color matches the jacket Pedro grabbed from the store. Is this affectionate act of touching the animal real or just a performance? Does this thing even feel?

"I'm going to walk back with Luna, back to where our other friend is. We can continue to talk from there." Pedro's heart is about to come out of his body. He takes tiny, shallow breaths.

Luna stares at the photo of her cousin being held up by the Visitor. She looks to the Visitor and then back to the picture. Pedro understands her desperate need

to connect with this fake Tasha, to communicate, as sur-
real and disturbing as it may be.

"I need you to focus, Luna," Pedro says. "Look at me
right now."

Luna finally turns to him. Her eyes convey a wave of
guilt. But doesn't Luna see this is not family? She doesn't
owe this fake Tasha a thing.

There is a noise somewhere in the distance. It's hard
to decipher where exactly the sound is coming from, but
Pedro hears it. The crackling of a radio. Shuffling of boots
on the ground. A group is heading their way.

"Come on!" Rafa yells. He springs from inside the
store, the fire extinguisher at the ready like he's a brown
John McClane from *Die Hard*.

"No, wait!" Pedro yells, but it's too late.

CHAPTER 27

It happens the instant Luna touches the picture of Tasha. A pulsating charge enters her body as soon as her finger lightly brushes against the Visitor's hand.

Images rush into her brain like currents of water. Luna gasps as quick cuts inside her mind show her a violent journey from the stars. A dark, velvet sky, so deep and vast. Another cut, and the focus is on Earth. A broad disk. The view overwhelms Luna. How can something so beautiful be so fragile? A different type of sadness sweeps over her, one of profound awareness of her delicate place in the world. The sobering realization of how Earth is nothing but a speck, a tiny dandelion that can easily be blown away.

Incredible. Shooting stars streak across the surface of the earth. Thunderstorms appear. This celestial brilliance can barely be captured on film, and Luna is being allowed to experience Earth as a wondrous oasis. Her body almost gives out because of the heaviness and the marvel.

Another cut, and Luna experiences the entrance into Earth's atmosphere. The landing. The meeting of the park ranger. His heart. A view of the Griffith Observatory. Luna's body jolts from each shot the security guard shoots. And finally, the picture of Tasha right there on the floor. The image infiltrates the Visitor, becomes a part of it. The Visitor, now Tasha, walking down a path. Then, there is the meeting with Rafa. The empty house becomes a living thing, a jungle. And the animals! The animals change, transform into something new. Grotesque and in pain.

"It's too much," Luna says to the Visitor. "I don't know if I can handle any more."

Luna touches her forehead and closes her eyes. The visions circulate so quickly, she can barely stand. But there is one image that stands out. It is of Tasha on her hospital bed, too weak to hold the phone. Luna on the other line, swearing to do the right thing.

Promise me.

Luna cries out, "Stop!"

The swirling images die down in her mind, but they don't stop altogether. As she tries to bring herself to the present, Luna concentrates on Pedro's lips and how he yells at her to join them. A few steps away, Rafa sprays at the lions with the fire extinguisher. The lions by the Visitor sit up and emit a low rumbling. They slowly hitch on their haunches, ready to attack.

Luna is cracking inside. She's at the very edge of seeing her friends mauled to death. This is no vision.

"Don't hurt them," she cries out. "Please don't hurt my friends!"

Seconds go by. A beat. Another.

"Strange," the Visitor finally says in that detached voice. "The three continue to protect each other."

Without any visible indication from the Visitor, the lions stop growling. The animals move away from them and trot into the darkness.

"Come on!" Pedro yells to Luna, but vines have circled her ankles, cuffing her. She tries to break free, but the harder she pulls, the tighter the hold becomes.

Then another voice joins the hysteria.

"Hands up!" someone yells.

LAPD officers enter the mall with their weapons drawn. Two police officers shout at Pedro and Rafa to drop to the ground and place their hands on the back of their heads. The longer they refuse to comply, the angrier the cops become.

"Don't shoot!" Rafa says. "We are not with her!"

"I said down to the ground! Right now!" the cop yells, inching closer to the two boys. Their guns are cocked, pointed only at Pedro and Rafa.

"*They* will not protect the three," the Visitor says.

This has happened before. The thought lodges itself in Luna's mind right in the middle of the dizzying visions. Two years ago, when the young boy was killed by cops, the video of the murder was played everywhere. The proof was there for everyone to see, but still, justice was never served. And there were many more untimely deaths caused by unchecked violence. So many more. Never ending.

Here is Luna, witnessing it in real time, unable to hide behind a call from her cousin urging her to take action, to join those on the streets against people with guns and their desire to suppress instead of listen.

Not again, Luna says to herself. She did nothing last time. Never joined the protests. Never lifted a finger even when her cousin's last wish was for her to do so. Instead, Luna brushed away her commitment to Tasha and hung out with Isaac because it was easier. Isaac and that circle of friends weren't paying attention to the action taking place in the streets. They kept everything light and silly, which was just what Luna needed, but the guilt never left. It only grew inside her, especially after Tasha was gone. Here she is, once again at a crossroads.

Pedro and Rafa cower. The cops circle in front of them, screaming. Luna can't stand and watch this slaughter come to fruition.

"You will fucking listen to me!" a cop yells. His boot presses against Rafa's back, and Rafa winces from the pain.

Luna turns to the Visitor. "Don't let the cops hurt them. Stop them."

The Visitor doesn't have to acknowledge her. Luna can't explain it, but she knows the Visitor will act.

The police officers focus on what's in front of them, failing to protect their backs. Giant, hybrid cougars with their branch horns quietly meet the cops in the rear. The beasts settle back on their hind legs, ready to leap forward. When the officers notice the lions, it's too late.

Hundreds of cougars launch onto their bodies, tearing into flesh. The confusion is immediate. Bullets ricochet about. Pedro drapes himself over Rafa while Luna eyes the destruction before her. The regret she has lived with for these past two years slowly melts away and a scary yet thrilling feeling emerges. Back then, young people led a movement to force the cops to account for their violent deeds, but they refused to acknowledge their guilt. Now the savagery the cops have always used as a tool to maintain power is being turned on them. For once the cops are unable to fight back and are forced to submit. A tiny hint of glee in witnessing this brutal reversal blossoms within Luna, but only for a second.

"Oh my god," she whispers as the screams and unnatural sounds amplify throughout the mall. Luna tries to detach herself from the horror. How the police officers are in anguish. How their protective gear is no match for these animals. But the violence is too much.

"No more," she screams. "Enough! Enough!"

"This is the only language acceptable to them," the Visitor says.

"Not everyone speaks this language," Luna says through tears.

The Visitor grins at Luna. The smile is exactly Tasha, and this frightening sight brings Luna to her knees. This fake Tasha is an inverted person so familiar, a disturbing nightmare come true. The Visitor rubs the ear of a lion closest to it, and with that gesture, the attack ends.

"It won't be long," the Visitor says. The vines keeping Luna trapped fall away. "The others will arrive."

"And us? What will happen?" Luna sobs. "I won't leave them."

The Visitor displays the same blank expression.

"Strange," it says. "The three continue to seek each other."

This fake copy of her cousin doesn't understand compassion or true human connection. It is a thing cosplaying as a human, a form who wears a skin.

It says, "The two will not be harmed."

Luna is in tears. Her heart racing. Rafa and Pedro lie still on the ground. *What do I do? Do I stay with them? Tasha, give me a sign.*

"The others will not understand your attachment to the two," the Visitor says. "This behavior goes against reason. The three continue to act unhampered. Each one a deviation."

Luna catches the tiniest hint of surprise in the Visitor's voice. It's the first time she is actually able to listen, unclouded by the strong desire to find her cousin. It's not Tasha's voice she's hearing but the sound of the mall's recorded announcement being mimicked back to her like a parrot. Even in the superficial tone, Luna can extract the Visitor's uncertainty. It's surprised by their actions and how they continue to help each other. Are they an anomaly to this thing? *A variable.* The thought returns to Luna. They *must* be.

The Visitor moves past the fallen cops. Cougars tag along as if they are following a galactic pied piper leading them to a promised land.

Luna knows she must stay close. A radical change is about to be imposed on this planet, and to hide from it is to be complicit. She won't be complicit again. She must do something. Luna gets up and follows the Visitor.

How will she survive this? How will they all?

CHAPTER 28

Rafa is slow to move, scared of what will greet him if he does. Pedro stirs beside him, and that gives him a bit of courage.

"Hey?" he whispers, unsure if noise will attract the beasts. "Are you okay?"

Pedro faces him and nods. "Yes, I am."

They detangle themselves from the floor and take in the chaos around them. The cop who bore down on Rafa's back lies still a few feet away from them. Farther down, someone moans in pain. Another cries out for help.

"Jesus Christ," Pedro says. "Where is she?"

Luna and the Visitor are nowhere in sight. Neither are the animals. Rafa is not upset by this revelation. Luna is dangerous, and he must protect himself.

"We can probably catch up to them," Pedro says.

"I'm not doing that." Rafa quickly gathers what he can of his belongings. There is no way he's going after Luna. She aligned herself with a thing that makes no sense. Rafa needs to be with his family.

"What do you mean? Where are you going?" Pedro says. "It didn't hurt us or Luna. Didn't you see that? This is a door opening for us. We have to find a way to stop it."

Rafa's anger pulses, but unlike Pedro, he doesn't want to argue. There is no reason for him to follow it. Rafa has already seen the hint of what's to come, and he doesn't need to see any more. He wants to spend what little hours he has left with Mónica, not on some suicide mission.

"Are you listening to me?" Pedro says again, but Rafa walks toward an exit.

"Stop telling me what to do," he says. "Go yourself. I'm not going to endanger myself for your friend."

Pedro yanks at Rafa's arm. "She's *our* friend. You are not living in a bubble anymore. You can't just stay on the sidelines, not after all we've seen. I won't let you."

The moans coming from the fallen cops echo in the mall's eerie silence. Noises reminding Rafa that he is about to find himself in a similar predicament if he continues.

"No." He turns away. "My family needs me."

"You won't have a family! Don't you get it? More are going to come," Pedro yells. "Even my trash family who can't stand me won't have much of a chance. It's on us to do something!"

Rafa ignores him and continues walking to the exit. But before he gets there, Pedro slams into his back and tackles him to the ground. They tussle on the floor, Rafa trying his best to pull away without hurting Pedro. He understands Pedro's frustration and anger, but what can they possibly do? It's hopeless.

Rafa finally pushes him off.

"We have no power!" he yells. "We are nothing."

A few seconds go by before Pedro slowly stands up. His face is filled with anguish.

"You're wrong, Rafa," Pedro says. "Why do you think everyone is so afraid of us? The cops, our teachers, my uncle, even this *thing* can't figure us out. We have to at least try. Luna might be the key."

"Or maybe we will be strangled to death by vines," Rafa says. He refuses to lie to himself that this Visitor's behavior is anything but an elaborate hoax. A big old trap to lure them to certain death.

"We are the only three people who have communicated with that alien. You, me, and Luna," Pedro says. "It means something, or it means nothing. Don't you want to find out which it is?"

Rafa grimaces at his words. "We are not saviors. All I can do is tend to my family, that's the only thing that matters."

"*We* are your family too!" Pedro exclaims. "I'm tired of circling around this. We are a dysfunctional family forced to deal with problems we didn't even create. To work together. What use will you be to them if we don't at least try?"

After a few seconds, Pedro holds his hand out and waits for Rafa to take it.

After the pandemic began, no one would touch each other. Rafa was lucky. He had Mónica. She was small back then, and they lived in a converted garage, squeezed in such close living quarters. They had each other. They survived.

Rafa looks at Pedro. Why does it feel so long ago, years ago even, when he first entered the classroom? Everyone glared at him, but it was Pedro he noticed. Pedro alerted him of the empty seat behind him. It wasn't much of a welcome, but it was better than nothing. A sliver of kindness.

A dysfunctional family? Rafa only knows bits and pieces of Pedro's life, less so for Luna. Taking Pedro's hand is acknowledging a part of Rafa that he wants to keep hidden. A barrier he's erected around him for protection. To survive on the daily without a home, to be constantly on the defense means you can't trust anyone. Still, Pedro and Luna are bound to him whether he likes it or not. Rafa is afraid, but what is the point of being with his family if he misses the chance to actually do something life changing, to take a course that will forever alter those he loves?

He grasps Pedro's hand and is surprised when Pedro pulls him close. They hold each other's stare for a few heartbeats and in that rare moment, Rafa feels serenity sweep over him.

The moment is broken by a rustling noise beside them. *The beasts.*

Rafa's heart takes off as mountain lions approach. But the animals do not charge. Instead, one circles Pedro's legs and rubs its head on his pants. Both boys are frozen in horror.

The lion eventually trots a couple of feet away from them, then turns as if beckoning them forward. Neon-colored leaves fall on the ground from the animal's sides. Another cougar does the same to Rafa.

"We're actually going to follow mountain lions," Rafa says.

"You got any other ideas?" Pedro says. "I'm just waiting for that cat to turn around and yell at us to hurry the hell up."

They head to the mall's stairwell.

"Be careful." Rafa helps Pedro when he almost trips over a step. How strange that their relationship has changed so much in such a short time. Even when Pedro fought with him, Rafa knew the anger was more about wanting him to stop being so self-centered.

But isn't that the American way, to only look out for yourself? What if now is the time to look beyond that? What if Pedro and Rafa are what a transformation should embody?

"There they go," Rafa says. "We better catch up."

"Okay."

The two follow the mountain lions across the parking lot, the mall exit just ahead. Outside, Los Angeles is a mad swirl of sirens. Helicopters take over the sky. Ambulances rush across the city while more men in uniform run into the mall. Pedro and Rafa hide behind a parking lot structure while the mountain lions stop a few feet ahead of them. Rafa closes his eyes as the other lions gruesomely attack the cops, creating a path for them to exit.

"Oh god," Pedro says from behind their barrier. "I don't know about this."

"We walk fast and stick close to the lions. On the count of three," Rafa says and begins the countdown. On three, they make their move, walking swiftly, doing their best to block out the bloodbath. The lions take a side street heading north, away from the busy boulevard.

Pedro pulls out his camera to capture the creeping vines visibly encroaching on homes. Unusual vegetation consumes the windows of a modern, two-story house, and the one next to it. He posts the video on his stories.

"Where do you think they're taking us?" he eventually asks, shouting against the din made from the helicopters.

"To the end of the world," Rafa says.

"Glendale?"

The laugh is needed, more than Rafa had expected. Every inch of his body is a ball of anxiety. "Maybe you should ask them."

"I may speak a ton of languages, but I don't speak Animorphs," Pedro says.

"You got jokes. Even now?"

"Jokes are the only way to survive," he says, and they press on.

This thing with Pedro? Rafa doesn't want to dwell on trying to define it, but right now he's the only thing that makes sense.

"What is that?" Rafa stops and grabs Pedro to alert him of this new find. A black crow unlike any they've ever seen blocks the street with the wide expanse of its wings. The tip of its beak flourishes a bright-red flower.

"Even with all this change, how in the world will that crow feed itself with a flower jutting from its mouth?" Pedro asks.

"It looks as awkward and lost as we are," Rafa says.

"At least we still have our limbs."

"But for how long?" Rafa says.

The crow hops over to the side of the sidewalk. Another soon joins him. The cougars continue trotting north.

"My parents used to assemble bouquets to sell on the side of the road in front of the cemetery," Rafa says. "They still have the scars on their hands from preparing them. I hate flowers. I bet that crow hates them too."

As if it's agreeing with Rafa, the crows makes an unnatural caw, booming as if the sound is amplified by hundreds of speakers.

"While our guide leads us to what will most likely be our death," Pedro starts, "any suggestions as to how we might be able to survive this?"

Rafa shakes his head. "This was your idea, not mine."

"What do you think, gatito? Do you understand English? How should we proceed? Meow once if you got an idea, two if you are as fucked as we are!" Pedro shouts. The cougar is a few feet ahead of them. "Maybe we're the flowers being plucked for display—"

A giant coyote, as big and fearsome as a bear, appears from in between two cars. Before Rafa can even take a breath to scream, the coyote pounces on Pedro, knocking him down. Saliva drips from its protruding jaw, menacing teeth grinding.

CHAPTER 29

People from the neighborhood ignore the two young girls walking in the middle of the street, having not yet seen the caravan of beasts trotting behind them. When the unusual animals jump atop parked cars, that is when the screams begin.

Luna stays focused on the Visitor, keeping up with its pace and ignoring the violence behind her. The chaos is a cinematic background full of fury, like a video game she does not want to play. Luna knows she must try to engage with the Visitor, to have it reveal anything that might be useful. Time is limited. This door is open only for so long as the fake Tasha allows her access. There's no room for selfishness. This unbelievable moment is bigger than Luna.

"Renewal," the Visitor says. The voice no longer sounds like the Beverly Center's PA system. It sounds exactly like Luna.

"If it's for renewal, then you must have been here before. Or at least the others have," Luna says, desperate to connect the dots as the Visitor leads them to their final destination.

Renewal, Luna thinks. She recalls what Pedro said at the observatory before the fight. The idea of planets being colonized. Isn't this the same thing? Newcomers trying to "civilize" the "savages" while taking over the land. *We're the savages.*

"We don't have a choice, do we?" Luna says. "This is going to be your home, whether we like it or not."

They take a left on Franklin Avenue. The Visitor barely speaks, although Luna continues to ask questions. It's hard for Luna to focus with the visions that flood her mind. They are like quick electrical pulses. Uncomfortable blasts into her brain she wishes she could shut off. One vision is constant though: the fleet of ships covering the skies paired with Tasha's voice asking Luna to keep her promise.

Luna sees groups of people dining at small round tables without a care in the world, as if what's happening less than a fifteen-minute drive away doesn't have a thing to do with them. The air is chilly, but heating lamps dot the already crowded strip of restaurants and boutique clothing stores. The bystanders laugh and continue with their conversations, until one person screams. And then another. But their shrieks are not in connection with the beasts following Luna and the Visitor. There is a new fear.

Luna inhales.

Coyotes spring up from the darkness with their jaws

protruding an unusual length. Their ears fan out even longer. Bodies as big as bears. Luna starts to hyperventilate. She was getting used to the lions, and now she has to deal with coyotes too? It is as if the dinosaurs have returned and Los Angeles citizens are encountering a real-life Jurassic Park.

Diners rush inside, abandoning their plates of food. The giant hounds topple over the tables. Their barks are otherworldly, demonic. The Visitor stops to take in the violent display with a glazed expression Luna is unable to decipher. Above it, palm trees start to sway aggressively. Their fronds fall down, covering the sidewalk and streets. Flowers in their neat plant boxes break free, growing larger, expanding. Luna holds her breath, afraid of what will happen next. Another innocent person to be torn apart by this thing, to be swallowed by the contaminating foliage.

The menacing coyotes straddle the heating lamps, sending them crashing to the ground in a burst of flames. A lamp lands by the Visitor, and it turns away from the fire. It actually flinches. The movement is so slight, barely noticeable, but it happened. It happened! Luna clings to this new revelation. *Fire.*

She scours the area for anything to use, but what? She doesn't have a lighter. Nothing to test her theory. But there is a possibility, and that is more than she's had since this nightmare began.

Luna glances around frantically, searching for something, anything, that can help her. She spots a hostess's podium standing abandoned, with a glass bowl full of matchboxes perched on top. *This is it.* The Visitor is only a few steps ahead of Luna. *It's now or never.* She digs her hand into the glass bowl. A giant coyote barks at her attempt, startling her enough that she knocks the bowl to the ground. The animal crashes into the podium, and splinters of wood rain down. It growls at Luna, ready to attack.

"Tasha!" Luna yells, but the Visitor seems absorbed with the advancing plants. Saliva runs down the massive coyote's mouth. Its eyes glowing unnaturally. Luna doesn't move an inch, her heart in her throat. The beast snarls at her.

Suddenly, a mountain lion swipes at the coyote with its paw, and the two begin to scrap. Luna runs to the Visitor, two matchboxes shoved into her pocket.

Luna almost hugs the Visitor on instinct, a reflex from being confronted with such a familiar face, but stops short. Those eyes are not really Tasha's. Luna must remind herself this thing isn't human.

"Why haven't you killed me yet?" Luna asks. "Are the memories I felt also in you? Is that why?"

"The encoding, or the 'memory' as you say, doesn't matter. The three humans presented a deviation, and with that came curiosity," the Visitor states. "Everything will turn, especially you."

Luna's sorrow is soon replaced with anger. Although the Visitor can easily pierce her heart, tear her body apart, it hasn't. Luna has finally figured out the reason why. The Visitor didn't expect much from its pets, only obedience.

But Luna is no pet.

Luna's been struggling all this time, trying to find the connection that binds her to this demon. She wanted to believe there was something benevolent about it. That Tasha was still in there. The truth is this thing is desecrating her cousin's soul. There is nothing good inside, no matter how hard Luna tries to find it.

An uprising doesn't have to be a mass movement. It only needs a single person. Maybe this is the start of one.

Up ahead, the Griffith Observatory stands stoic against a dark, cloudless sky.

CHAPTER 30

Another mutated coyote appears to the left of Rafa, gnashing its pointy teeth. Fear keeps Rafa's feet cemented to the ground, while steps away from him lies Pedro, cringing while gnarly claws pierce his skin. He screams.

"Please, don't hurt us," a desperate Rafa says. "We didn't do this to you."

He knows his pleas are useless, but what else is there to do? To avoid conveying a threat to the coyotes, he glances up to the dark October sky filled with so many brilliant stars. He recalls the last time he gazed at the clouds with his sister, a day spent at the Tar Pits.

"Why did the elephants get stuck?" Mónica asked.

"The mammoths used to live here thousands of years ago. The tar bubbled up, and they probably didn't know what it could do to them. They became extinct, like the dinosaurs," he said. "It happens."

Rafa nudged Mónica to try to imagine what the city looked like back then. Giant animals roaming the LA streets. He remembered feeling small and insignificant.

Thinking how one false step and he too could be stuck forever. Like now.

The coyote nearest him barks, drawing closer. Rafa bows his head, tries to make himself smaller.

"Please," he begs. Their guides, the mountain lions, keep their distance as if they don't want to be involved. The giant hounds edge closer and closer.

Rafa sneaks a glance to the middle of the street, where the immense coyote hovers over the cowering Pedro. *What can I do to save him?* No one deserves this ending, not Pedro or Rafa. Like the animals, they too are victims. Objects being used in an unimaginable war. Rafa searches his mind, desperate for a way out of this. Then he directs his attention to the coyote atop of Pedro.

"Get off him," Rafa says in a firm voice, the same one he uses to get his sister's attention, the same he used on the Dolce & Gabbana clerk.

The coyote turns to him and lets out a yip. It nuzzles against Pedro's face then suddenly pulls away. The animal by Rafa bows its large head to sniff the ground and soon joins the other. With caution, Rafa walks to Pedro, who hasn't moved, his eyes shut.

"They are gone. The coyotes," Rafa says in as steady a voice as he can muster. "You are okay. Pedro. Open your eyes."

Pedro covers his face and cries.

"I can't take this," he says.

Rafa kneels down beside him. "It's okay. I'm here. I won't leave, no matter what."

Pedro's hands are trembling, so Rafa covers them with his own.

"Just tell me when you are ready to stand, and I will help you," he says.

"What if I can't? What if this is all I can do?" Pedro sounds so broken that it layers another fear onto Rafa. He doesn't want to lose him. Rafa slowly caresses Pedro's shoulder. He will stay here for as long as it takes.

"We do this together," he says. "It's just us two and some lions and a coyote and a weird-looking crow."

Pedro laughs a bit then cries again.

"Like in a dystopian *Wizard of Oz*," he says in between sobs.

"Something like that."

After a moment, Pedro gets up.

"I don't know if I can walk," he says, embarrassed.

"Sure you can. Small steps." Rafa brushes a lingering tear from Pedro's cheek. "The coyote is a couple of feet ahead. There are a few behind us too."

Pedro still doesn't move. Drops of blood seep through his shirt where the coyote tore into him. Rafa pulls out his handkerchief and presses against the wound to stop the bleeding. It takes a moment but it works.

"Let's breathe, okay." Rafa inhales deeply. Pedro follows. Then they both exhale. They do it three times until Pedro no longer has a shaky voice.

"Okay," Pedro says. He leans into Rafa. "I think I can do this."

Pedro's eyes widen when he's finally able to see the

coyote in all its monstrosity. The streets are eerily quiet, and he whispers, "Animal Crossing gone wild." Rafa snorts. He wraps his arm around Pedro, happy to see his humor back. When he does, Pedro leans in and kisses his cheek.

"Thank you," he says with such tenderness.

"You're welcome," Rafa says and heat rises on his face. The walls he's constructed around him his whole life dissolve, and he wonders if Pedro will mark this location as the place they fell in love.

"Ready?" he eventually says.

The animals head toward the Hollywood Hills. It is getting darker and harder for them to keep up. It's not until Pedro uses his cell phone's flashlight that they are able to continue.

"I thought I knew Los Angeles, but it doesn't look recognizable to me," Pedro says. "It's as if we're entering a place that existed in another time. We definitely don't belong here."

"Or maybe we do. Why would these animals continue to lead us through this? Sure, the coyote tried to eat you at first but it eventually licked your face. Did you notice?"

"No, I was too busy trying not to die," Pedro says and suddenly stops. "Why are you so calm? Why haven't you broken down?"

"I don't know. Maybe because I'm not alone," Rafa says. "Maybe because I'm with you." This time, it's Pedro who acts a little shy, but Rafa gently squeezes his hand.

There is a break in the path, and they can finally see their destination. The observatory is brightly lit, a white building just up the deserted path, shining down on them.

"Do you think Luna's up there?" Pedro asks.

"I hope so, or all of this walking is for nothing," Rafa says.

The two follow the beasts up various zigzagging trails leading to the observatory. As the denseness of the park becomes too intense, Rafa makes sure Pedro is always only a touch away.

CHAPTER 31

Two patrol cars block the small parking lot located in front of the Griffith Observatory. LAPD is on high alert with all the unexplainable incidents occurring across the city. Officer Matthew Hernandez wishes they had sent him to Hollywood where things are really heating up instead of this babysitting gig.

"Been thinking about renting a cabin in Lake Arrowhead for the weekend," he says to his partner, Brian. "Taking the newborn. Have you been there? It's nice."

Brian nods but doesn't add anything to the conversation. A couple of days ago, Brian told Matthew he spoke too much after he shared another story about the cute things baby Mateo does in the mornings. Ever since then Matthew's been trying to keep to himself, but that's not his way. He's always been a talker. It's the one thing he likes about the job, being able to talk to people one on one.

"Yeah, the lake would be nice, although it might be a little cold," he says more to himself than to his partner, who turns to face the building. "Cindy and I always rented a place there. Sometimes you need to get away from the city."

He doesn't like his work partner, and Matthew is positive the feeling is mutual. Brian should have retired by now, but word around the precinct is he's been planting evidence for years. Community got wind of it when a young Black boy was taken into custody, and they didn't relent until Brian was forced to take a desk job. Now Matthew has to deal with this old man's anger while trying to find his footing as a rookie. It's nothing new. He just has to wait this out until he proves himself. Keep his nose clean and make those connections.

Matthew rests his hand on his belt, stretches his neck, and does a squat. He wonders how long they will have to stay up here. At least it's quiet. No one is really visiting the observatory, not at this hour. They haven't had any issues. It's only been an hour, and most of the stragglers took note and quickly left.

From where the cop is, he could see the city's skyline from atop the Griffith Observatory at night. He checks to see if his partner is paying attention and sneaks a photo of the brilliant skyline. Matthew gives a nod to the other police officers as they patrol the far end of the parking lot. They're rookies like him. Earlier, when Matthew joked around with one of them, Brian sent them off to patrol. The man is so full of hate.

Brian whistles. Someone approaches the parking lot. As the dark figures pass a street lamp, Matthew sees it's two young girls, both in their late teens.

"Yeah, I'm on it," he says while his partner continues to lean on the patrol car.

"Ladies, you're not allowed up here. The observatory is closed," Matthew says. His hand still rests on his belt. It's late for these girls. He thinks about how his parents would let him go out at all hours of the night while his sisters stayed home. Cindy and he talked about having a girl, but boys are easier to raise—case in point, these two right here. "Got to turn right around and head back down the hill."

"I beg you to let us through," one of the girls say, the one with long dark hair. "Please. She won't stop."

"Well, I'm telling you to stop right there. Both of you." The rookie cop reaches down to the side where his gun is. The response is automatic. It's what he's been trained to do all those hours at the academy. To demand respect. What Matthew is unable to see is how a vine from the corner of the park is slithering over to him. Other plants are doing the same, making their way to his partner.

"Turn right around, and head back down, or I'm going to have to take you in," he says. Matthew shrugs at Brian, who suddenly comes to attention.

"Hands up right the fuck now!" Brian yells. Matthew changes gear and pulls out his gun too.

"Stop hurting people," the brunette says while the one with pink hair continues to move forward.

"Don't move," Matthew yells. The landscape draws nearer.

"Enough! You can't continue doing this. I won't let you!" The girl yanks at the pink-haired girl, but within seconds she is sent flying, not by a push but by something else. Something Matthew can't see.

"What the f—"

A branch tears into Matthew's leg and blood gushes out. He drops to the ground. His gun is snatched from his belt and buried in the dirt while Brian is dragged across the parking lot. Plants encircle Matthew's body. He tries to grab the bumper of the patrol car, trying to prevent the same fate as his partner, but it's impossible. He's soon trapped against a tree, thorns piercing his wrists, his ankles, his neck.

"My god," Matthew says.

The girl with pink hair walks ahead, fixated on reaching the building. It takes a few minutes, but eventually the girl on the ground gets up and goes to him. Blood trickles on the side of her head. The girl tries to break him free, to rip at the vines. But with every one she is able to take out, another appears.

"I got a baby," he cries. "Please help me."

Matthew becomes frantic. He needs to survive this, to see Mateo and Cindy again.

"I don't know what to do," the girl says. "Don't you see? She's controlling all of this."

"Backup. Call for . . ."

Leaves enter his mouth, gagging him. He can no longer speak. The girl cries out in pain.

"I'm sorry," she says. "I'm so sorry."

There's nothing she can do. She's just a kid. A young kid.

Panic sets in, but he has to fight against it. He needs to calm down. To think this through. The girl gets up, weeping hysterically. Matthew watches her walk away, leaving him there.

CHAPTER 32

Luna crouches down against a pristine white wall, the entrance to the observatory just above. Her hands are bloody, skin torn. There is a gash on the side of her head. Warm blood oozes down, and she feels light-headed. The facade is providing her only support.

She didn't plan to attack the Visitor. Not at all. Then again, everything Luna's done since this began has been impulsive. She had to do something. She couldn't be a docile witness to the violent actions being taken.

Everything will turn, the Visitor said.

The words crawled inside of her. With each step they took toward the observatory, Luna tossed the statement around. What it means to turn, to be used against your will. The alien's only mission is to begin the process, but that doesn't mean Luna had to stand by and do nothing. So she attacked the Visitor, and the plants did what they've been doing. They struck her down.

She cradles her head, digs in her backpack to find a piece of clothing, anything, to stop the bleeding. Luna grabs several tissues and presses them against the injury, moaning from the pain.

The officer said to call backup. She pulls out her phone, only to discover there's barely a charge left. There are so many unanswered messages. Old messages from Soledad. Various texts from Pedro. Many from her mother. She dials the number, but the call goes directly to voice mail.

"Mom, my phone is about to die." Luna wavers, unsure how to proceed. She can picture her mother in the hospital, overwhelmed by the amount of people hurt. "I don't know how to say this, but they're coming from the sky. From outer space. They'll be here soon. Take shelter. I love you, Mom. I love you so much. Just remember I love you with all my heart."

Luna starts to cry, her emotions unable to be contained. She doesn't think there is a way out of this. Before the last bars of her phone disappear, she sends a text to Pedro and Rafa alerting them of where she is.

Please come, she texts.

* * *

In the hospital, Luna's mother argues with a doctor who refuses to believe her. How the injuries seem to echo each other. This isn't the first argument she's had today. Doctors, especially male doctors, just assume nurses aren't smart enough. They don't get that they are the first ones to see the patients, to take their vitals, to ask the right questions.

"Stop dismissing what my coworkers and I are

telling you," she says. "These patients are all suffering from protrusions caused by branches. All of them."

The doctor smirks, like a pompous know-it-all, and she wants to slap him. Instead, she mutters to herself while walking away.

"No, there's no more room. Keep them in the hallway," she yells at an aide.

Patients crowd the floor. More and more arrive. She has had no break, no lunch, not a moment to speak to her daughter. Her baby girl. She tries Luna one more time, but as soon as the phone connects, Ceci calls to her from one of the occupied rooms.

"He's got some sort of allergic reaction," Ceci says. The patient's skin bubbles.

"Call Poison Control," Luna's mom shouts. "Right now!"

* * *

As Pedro and Rafa enter the Griffith Observatory's parking lot, they find cops with leaves covering their mouths. Their eyes wildly jet about, begging for relief.

"Híjole," Pedro says.

They both tread cautiously through the lot, the heaviness of the night pressing down on them. There is no need to declare it publicly. Every step they take to the observatory is also a step toward a future that they will most likely not be a part of.

"They must be near," Rafa says. "Let's take it slow."

* * *

Mónica doesn't want to go back to sleep, no matter what Vickie tells her. Instead, the little girl stands by the window. Vickie thought it would be a good idea to invite her to sleep in her room. Mónica's been distraught ever since her family arrived at their house. The gesture worked at first, and the little girl was able to nod off for an hour. But she's up again.

"I want Rafa," Mónica says.

"He'll be back in the morning," Vickie says, although she has no idea. His parents have tried reaching him, but there's been no answer. The riot that happened at his school seems to have branched off into different parts of the city like a contagious disease. Vickie's tried to follow the action on TikTok, but it's been so confusing. Some blame a girl with pink hair for starting the violence. Some say it's a group of kids. Others have no idea what's happening. Church members will be gathering tomorrow. There's too much uncertainty, and joining together will help quell some of it.

"Mónica, come to bed. You must be so tired," Vickie says. Mónica refuses. If only Rafa would call, send word, anything. Vickie's worried too.

"Do you want to draw? Rafa told me you like drawing." Vickie finds crayons and blank sheets of paper. She lays them out on the floor. Two sheets, one for Mónica and one for her. "Come. We can draw for a little bit. Maybe that will help."

Mónica is reluctant to join Vickie, but eventually she does. She grabs a blue crayon and paints a sky. She draws a house and the streets. She uses a yellow crayon for arrows to point to the house.

"What are you drawing?" Vickie asks.

"A map for Rafa."

✳ ✳ ✳

Pedro and Rafa find Luna cradling her head. She is a little dazed. Rafa offers her water, and it helps.

"You're bleeding," Pedro says. "You tried it, didn't you? That fucking bitch." He uses the cuff of his sleeve to wipe the blood.

"I saw things. Unimaginable things. I can't explain how or why, but I was able to see these visions," Luna says. "Ships appearing in the sky. So many of them."

She looks up as if searching for a confirmation that this devastating arrival is imminent.

"Then it's useless," Rafa says.

"No. I mean, maybe. I'm not sure," she says. "Fire. Maybe fire can hurt it."

"You only spent a few extra hours with that thing. Doesn't make you an expert," Pedro says. "Maybe Rafa is right. It's useless. We're going to risk our lives for a small possibility."

"We have to try." Luna says. "In a couple of hours, it won't make a difference. The Visitors are coming. The only difference will be where we are when those things land. This alien doesn't get to perform in my cousin's body. She's cosplaying a person I loved more than anything. I won't let it continue."

Rafa and Pedro are silent. They've come this far. The goal was always to find a crack, and maybe Luna has found one.

"Then let's burn this bitch," Pedro says.

CHAPTER 33

The Café at the End of the Universe. That is what the cafeteria located in the observatory is called, and Pedro thinks this is way too on the nose, even for him. He takes a picture of the sign. Although his phone is also about to die, he has to post something to his followers.

The caption reads: *Space aliens are about to land. This is not a joke.*

Above him, the roar of helicopters begins. It appears as if they are coming in from downtown, heading west. Pedro thinks about his mother. When he was young, he used to call helicopters "angry birds." His mother wouldn't correct him. To this day she still calls them that.

It wasn't always so bad, he thinks. There was definitely love between him and his mother, and Pedro chooses to let this thought guide him forward. As much as he hates his uncle, he knows the man will protect Pedro's mother. His uncle will curse Pedro's name till kingdom come, but at least his mother will not be alone.

To avoid the main entrance, Pedro joins Rafa and

Luna as they walk toward the back of the observatory. They enter the empty terrace where patrons can eat and take in the beautiful view of the city's skyline. Rafa carries a small jug of gasoline.

The glass doors are locked. Without hesitation, Pedro grabs a rock and breaks the window. The noise won't help their cause, but hopefully the helicopters will mask some of it. He kicks the remaining glass and kneels down to enter. The other two follow.

It's a terrible plan. They all agreed to it, but it's still pretty ridiculous. Rafa insisted if they were going to try to burn it, they would need more than just a couple of matches. Igniting fluid. Rubbing alcohol. Anything to get a real fire going. The patrol car was Luna's idea. In one of them, they located a funnel and plastic tubing. In another they found a jug. No one questioned how Rafa knew exactly how to syphon gasoline from the car.

"I'm surprised they don't have a blowtorch," Pedro said, rummaging through the trunk. "Didn't all my money from taxes go to high-tech weapons? Just . . . useless."

A first aid kit produced rubbing alcohol and gauze to help clean Luna up a bit. Pedro stored the kit in his bag. They thought about taking the rifle but figured it wouldn't make a difference.

Inside the cafe, the three fan out quickly. Pedro locates tumblers from a kiosk. He freezes when he hears a noise.

"You heard that?" he asks.

"It must be her," Luna says. "I mean, it. The Visitor."

She takes a tumbler from him and joins Rafa by a table. He takes the gasoline and pours it into the glasses emblazoned with the image of the Griffith Observatory.

"What else?" Luna asks.

"I think that's it," Rafa says. Luna hands Pedro a box of matches. The other, she holds. Pedro checks the café again. The kitchen. Anything that might be of use.

"We should go," Rafa says.

As Pedro walks past a table, he suddenly stops.

"Salt is evil," he says. The other two look on confused. "I just remembered something Mr. Reiña used to always say. Mr. Reiña owns La Plaza—it doesn't matter. He has a room overrun with house plants. He always said salt is evil for your body and for your plants. That's what he said."

"This?" Luna lifts a saltshaker from a table.

Pedro runs and gets another tumbler. He fills it with salt. Luna and Rafa help, grabbing the saltshakers from the other tables.

"Salt and gasoline," Luna says, staring at the cup. "We can't be serious."

"What else can we do? You said maybe fire. Well, I'm going to maybe season it with salt," Pedro says.

"What's the plan?" Rafa says, shaking his head. "Go up and offer her a drink. Salt? How?"

"You're asking me?" Pedro says, annoyed. "I don't know!"

"I'll pretend to drink from it," Luna says, mimicking taking a sip as if the demonstration will stop it from being so silly an action. "I go in first, to talk to it. You both sneak in, and when the time is right, we throw gasoline on it. Just act casual."

"Act casual. Are you kidding me right now?" Pedro cracks up because the absurdity of this plan is hitting him so hard. "This is such a mess."

He suddenly finds himself on the verge of tears, but he shakes his whole body to let it go. "Okay, let's just do it."

She smiles weakly at him.

"Wait," Pedro says. He pulls out his phone and starts recording.

"We are going to try salt and fire," he says into the camera. "Maybe it will work on this thing. Maybe not. Take care of yourself. I love you all."

Pedro posts the video.

Before they take the stairs, he wraps his arm around Rafa and then Luna.

"I love you both even though we barely know each other. I love you both, and I trust you to protect me," Pedro says. "And I promise to do the same."

"I promise," Luna says. "I love you too."

Rafa nods his head in agreement.

And Pedro chuckles. "Always the quiet one," he says and rests his head on Rafa's chest for a second. Then the three take to the stairs.

CHAPTER 34

The theater doors are wide open. Moss and dangling vines cover the ceiling. A sweet scent from a night-blooming jasmine fills the air. As agreed, Luna enters first, holding in her hand a cup of gasoline. It smells, and she hopes the floral fragrance masks the odor.

As she slowly walks in, she notices how every single seat is occupied with plants, except for one. The Visitor sits in the front row, watching the large screen as it plays a film about the cosmos. The movie is dated, from the eighties, the same one played during their field trip. The narrator of the film extols the exciting planetary stars and the vastness of the galaxy. Worlds almost impossible to fathom.

Luna is so afraid that she will collapse, that her knees will no longer support her. Her copy of a cousin sits before her, and Luna can't help but remember when they were rooted deep in those seats laughing uncontrollably. A beautiful memory of joy. Luna holds on to that vision, lets it flood her mind and push out the ugliness she's seen so far.

This thing is not part of her. Not blood. Not family.

"This isn't your true form. Will you show me what you really look like?" Luna asks. This is not part of the plan, and it's not what she expected to come out of her mouth. But the anger churning inside her just bursts out. How this fake Tasha used her cousin, used her like a strange puzzle it couldn't figure out.

"Eventually there will be a change" the Visitor says. Its voice now the voice of the narrator in the film. "And it won't make a difference what you or I look like."

The movie plays again.

"My task was to begin the process," the Visitor says. "To blanket the cities."

"We won't just bow down to what you want," Luna says. "We'll fight to keep this our home. You understand? You're not the first disease to try to wipe us out."

As Luna speaks, Pedro and Rafa enter the theater. They slowly creep to the front.

"The fight will be fascinating to witness," the Visitor says.

"Like a game?" Luna responds with disgust.

"No, not like a game," the Visitor says, its eyes still glued to the big screen. "Like a dialogue between species."

A dialogue? More like war, Luna thinks.

"You might refuse to answer this, but why us, why Pedro and Rafa? Why me?" Luna says. "I need to know. Are we special in some way?"

"To clear a path for the others to enter. To relay

information and sow seeds on the ground," the Visitor says. "Humans are predictable in action. They never sway. But the three never followed the template. The three deviated at every turn."

You didn't expect us, what we are capable of doing for each other. The three of us changed your plans somehow, Luna thinks, confident in her findings.

"You're not going to win, not if we can help it," she says.

This is the sign, their clue. Pedro and Rafa know the time to act is now.

Rafa empties the tumbler with salt on the Visitor, spilling most of it on its arm. The sizzling is not immediate, but soon the salt seeps into the skin, burning through it like acid. The Visitor doesn't cry out in pain. It looks down at the sizzling skin and back at Rafa. The hand is no longer a hand but a jellylike substance.

With the other, still-human hand, the Visitor grabs hold of Rafa's neck and squeezes tight. It lifts Rafa up; his feet dangle. Luna throws the gasoline on the Visitor. Pedro does the same then tries to help Rafa, who squirms in the air, struggling to breathe.

"Hurry!" Pedro screams. Vines circle around his body, pulling him away from Rafa. They puncture his skin, wrap around his neck. The smell of jasmine is choking.

"I can't. I can't do it!" Luna's hands are sweaty, and she can't light the matches. Her fingers are like giant thumbs. She tries again. Rafa's face is red. He won't hold on for much longer. A branch from a large, seated plant leans disturbingly forward like it's about to propel towards her.

At last, Luna's trembling fingers light a match and throw it in the direction of the Visitor. The fire quickly catches. The Visitor drops Rafa to the floor. Luna strikes another match and sets the plants in front of her aflame. Pedro escapes the vines and pulls Rafa away.

Fire engulfs the bucket seats while the Visitor flails. It makes no sound but still tries to reach out to Luna. The skin it occupied slowly disintegrates.

"Tasha," Luna cries out.

The last reminder of her cousin burns off, and Luna feels her heart breaking. She once again has to say goodbye, even if this Tasha was just a costume. The pain is somehow worse this time around, and nothing will ever be the same.

The movie continues to play as the theater fills with smoke. Scenes of vast galaxies not yet discovered. Planets with hints of life. Whole universes. And the optimistic narrator leads the viewers through it all.

"Exciting new worlds await you," the narrator says.

CHAPTER 35

The three stumble out of the observatory, coughing and gagging. Behind them, the blaze grows. The sky is still dark but strangely, birds are starting to chirp. In only a few hours, it will be day soon. A new day to mark the change that will be coming.

Far ahead, the cops are still tied to the trees. Down in the city, officials try to make sense of what's happening. They are not prepared. No one is.

One cougar, maybe the first one they met at the start of this adventure, lumbers over to where the three stand. There is a communication, a language being spoken between the animals. The extraordinary coyotes and birds shift their position to be behind the three, as if protecting them.

Luna grabs hold of Rafa's hand. Pedro takes Luna's.

The sky slowly turns colors. Menacing clouds suddenly appear. Soon the clouds will part to reveal the Visitors arriving to take over.

"We need to hide," Pedro says. He tugs on Rafa, who adds pressure to his grip.

"Let me see this," Luna says. "Only for a second, to believe it."

They stay and watch the clouds turn. Strange lights come into sight. Pedro wonders if the light from last week was the first sign. Or maybe there were many signs before. A whole conspiracy of lies meant to keep them in the dark.

They watch for only a few seconds more as the sky is littered with unusual activity. Hundreds of lights. It is a majestic and fearful sight to behold.

Rafa doesn't want to witness the immensity of this scene. How will he be able to describe such things to his sister when he finally sees her? The stories will be too much to convey. His sister's deep-brown eyes are just as fantastical. Her curiosity too. A tiny human so willing to see joy in the darkest places. Rafa must find his family so they can arm themselves against this new danger. He will borrow Pedro's phone to call them. The cities will be teeming with chaos. Perhaps heading south makes sense. They've always been a mobile family. They will need to find shelter in the spaces where families are ignored. Plenty of places where people like him are left to fend for themselves.

"I'm ready." Luna finally looks away.

"Never thought I would hate the observatory as much as I do now," Pedro says.

"We need a car and to go to where there's plenty of salt," Rafa says.

Luna thinks of her mother and when she will be able to see her again.

"Salt and gasoline," she says. "We've got to warn everyone."

In a very small nook nestled in the base of Luna's long neck, a tiny little structure punctures out of her skin. She is unable to feel it, not yet anyway. In fact, she will later think it is only a small pimple. But the alien skin structure will change, morph into something else. Something plantlike. It will only appear on Luna, not Pedro or Rafa. It doesn't belong on her body, but it will manifest itself within her anatomical structure.

A variable. Each of them an experiment.

The three enter the dense foliage. Soon they are completely hidden. No one can see them, only the animals that have grown used to them. The beasts follow along, letting the three lead the way this time.

ACKNOWLEDGMENTS

As I write this, there's a newspaper article on how the two richest men in the world are fighting over the moon, while the Pentagon released a report on UFOs. Sometimes reality is stranger than fiction. *We Light Up the Sky* is a classic alien invasion story, but it's also the story of how young people of color are overlooked and underestimated during times of crisis. I hope you love and root for Pedro, Luna, and Rafa.

Thanks to the amazing team at Bloomsbury, especially my editors Claire Stetzer and Mary Kate Castellani, and the talented artist Jor Ros for the beautiful cover design. Love always to my agent Eddie Schneider.

And a special shoutout to the teens following SpaceX *Falcon* four years ago who shared their findings with me, becoming inspiration for this novel.